OUTLAW LAND

Center Point
Large Print

Also by Bradford Scott and available from
Center Point Large Print:

The Slick-Iron Trail
Guns of the Alamo
Texas Rider
Powder Burn

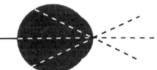

**This Large Print Book carries the
Seal of Approval of N.A.V.H.**

OUTLAW LAND
A Walt Slade Western

Bradford Scott

CENTER POINT LARGE PRINT
THORNDIKE, MAINE

This Center Point Large Print edition
is published in the year 2019 by arrangement with
Golden West Literary Agency.

Originally published in the US by Pyramid Books.

The text of this Large Print edition is unabridged.
In other aspects, this book may vary
from the original edition.
Printed in the United States of America
on permanent paper.
Set in 16-point Times New Roman type.

ISBN: 978-1-64358-202-3 (hardcover)
ISBN: 978-1-64358-206-1 (paperback)

Library of Congress Cataloging-in-Publication Data

Names: Scott, Bradford, 1893-1975, author.
Title: Outlaw land / Bradford Scott.
Description: Center Point Large Print edition. | Thorndike, Maine :
     Center Point Large Print, 2019. | Series: A Walt Slade Western
Identifiers: LCCN 2019008512| ISBN 9781643582023 (hardcover :
     alk. paper) | ISBN 9781643582061 (paperback : alk. paper)
Subjects: LCSH: Large type books.
Classification: LCC PS3537.C9265 O98 2019 | DDC 813/.52—dc23
LC record available at https://lccn.loc.gov/2019008512

OUTLAW LAND

1

From where he sat on the wide veranda of his big ranchhouse, old John Harper could see the dark smudge staining the blue of the Texas sky. Like an evil emanation, it hovered over Gunlock. His tufted brows drew together in a frown.

The frown grew blacker as a sound reached his ears, a thin, metallic wail that never came from the throat of prowling coyote or hunting wolf.

Harper swore and tugged his bristling mustache. The blasted oil town was bad enough, but a blankety-blank railroad was worse.

John Harper owned broad acres. For mile on mile extended his level rangeland, grown with needle and wheat grasses that would plump out the sides of a steer in no time. Mile on mile, bastioned on the northwest by the grim Cito Hills that shouldered their way across the Texas state line into New Mexico. To the south was the broken ruggedness of the Cap Rock, and beyond this was the beginning of the wild austerity of the big bend.

The Cito Hills were, and always had been, outlaw land. Sanctuary for hunted men, from which they raided, as had the Comanche before them.

Until recently, Harper had not been much bothered by the outlaws, who preferred to do their cow stealing elsewhere, out of respect for the nearly two-score able hands old John Harper had in his employ. The ordinary brush popper shied away from those cowboys who were more accurate with rifle and six-gun than the average.

Yes, it was wonderful cattle country. The prairie was dotted with groves and thickets, and the canyons scoring the lower slopes of the western hills provided shelter from the heat and the storms. John Harper, along with others of his kind, believed it should stay that way, and thought it always would.

But things were changing here as elsewhere in Texas, and the whole Southwest, for that matter. A different brand of owlhoots was making an appearance, and their depredations, including cow stealing, were not the hit-and-miss methods of their brush prowling predecessors. They conducted operations with efficiency and dispatch, their methods those of practical and hard-headed businessmen, which was just what they were. Harper, as well as his neighbors, began losing cattle, and the wideloopers were so skillful that so far his hands had been unable to run them down.

Lank Jim Sanborn, Harper's range boss, strolled out of the living room. Lank Jim grinned. Harper glowered, and turned his gaze back to that lowering smoke cloud to the south.

"Ain't no sense gettin' het up and pawin' sod."

advised Lank Jim. "Progress is progress and the wheels will keep on turnin' no matter how much sand you try to shovel into the gears."

Old John's wrath erupted in roaring profanity directed at the oil town, Lank Jim, and creation in general.

Lank Jim wasn't afraid of his irascible employer, or of anything else, for that matter. He just waited patiently for the explosion to cease, which it finally did, for lack of breath.

"You'll go off some time in a spell like that," Lank Jim predicted.

"It's a blasted outrage!" stormed old John. "I don't know what the section is comin' to. Bad enough when the blankety-blank nesters stole that land over to the east—"

"They bought it from the state and paid for it," Lank Jim interpolated.

"They had no business buyin' it!" bawled Harper. "That land was always open range and had oughta stayed that way."

"Yes, but just the same it was state-owned land," said Lank Jim. "I tried to talk you and the other boys into gettin' title to that land before somebody else slid in ahead of you, but you wouldn't listen—you had to be bullheaded and go your own way. So don't be bellerin' over what's your own fault."

"Even admittin', which I don't, that the nesters had a right to get title to the land, you know that when we heard of what was in the wind, I was already head over heels in debt from buyin' the Morton holding to the north, and I still am," Harper growled. "I wasn't in any position to buy."

"The land I advised you not to buy," interpolated Lank Jim. Harper swore again.

"I know what I would do," he added, scowling even more blackly. "I'd sell the whole south pasture if somebody would make me a decent offer. The blasted oil has ruined it."

Sanborn didn't believe it was so, but decided not to argue that particular point; nobody was likely to make an offer in this land-poor section where most of the owners already had more range than they could use. Also he knew how an old-time cowman hated to part with even an acre of his holding. Much as he needed money at the moment, it would take a mighty good offer to induce Harper to let that pasture go.

Harper snorted and rumbled. "The blasted nesters do seem to be behavin' themselves fairly well, though I still ain't sure where my cows are goin' or who's been wide-loopin' 'em, and I sure got my suspicions about that young squirt, Bill Carr. But that blankety-blank town down there! Those hellions are the scrapin' from the Devil's kettle. And the blankety-blank railroad brings 'em in."

"Are some off-color gents there," Lank Jim admitted. "But you have to expect that from any boom town like Gunlock, and if the railroad hadn't been built they'd have showed up anyhow."

"Those blasted-snortin' engines scare fat off the cows and gas from the blankety-blank oil wells pizen 'em," Harper growled. Lank Jim didn't think it worth while to argue the point. And just to keep the pot simmering, he vouchsafed a bit of bad news.

"Pretty sure we lost close onto fifty head from the northwest pasture last night," he remarked.

Harper's face turned purple and he breathed with apparent difficulty. But Lank Jim did not appear to notice these alarming symptoms; he continued, "We tracked 'em toward the hills, as usual, and there we lost the trail, as usual; there's no followin' 'em over those rocks, or at least we ain't had any luck so far."

"What am I payin' those work dodgers for, anyhow?" demanded Harper. "Why can't they keep watch over my property?"

Lank Jim shrugged his scrawny shoulders. "It ain't easy for even thirty-three hands to keep watch over all of a spread this size," he pointed out. "And men can't work all day and set up keepin' watch all night, too."

John Harper, a fair man despite his irascible disposition, nodded.

"Guess that's so," he admitted. "But Jim, the sidewinders are stealin' me blind."

"You ain't the only one," consoled Sanborn. "The other boys have been losin' cows, too. And folks beside cowmen are havin' trouble. And remember, the Medford stage was held up and robbed just a few nights ago. Driver shot. Hurt sorta bad, I'm scairt."

"Stage didn't have guards along?"

Sanborn shook his head. "Nobody was supposed to know it was packin' money; it don't often do it," he replied. "Guards would sorta say it was packin' money. The blasted owlhoots found out some way—seem able to find out anything."

Harper shook his head. "Things are a mess," he growled. "Well, maybe those letters I wrote will get some results. Ain't heard anything so far.

"And," he added with apparent irrelevance, "I still got notions about that blasted Bill Carr over to the east; I got a feeling his herd grows too fast."

"Now hold it!" protested Sanborn. "Because you don't happen to agree with a feller doesn't necessarily mean there's something off-color about him."

Harper subsided to growls and rumbles and didn't argue the point further. But Sanborn had a feeling he hadn't changed his opinion.

Yes, things in and around Gunlock were in a considerable mess. Which was why Ranger Walt Slade, named by the Mexican *peones* of the Rio Grande river villages *El Halcón*—The Hawk—rode into Gunlock as the lovely blue dusk was sifting down from the western hills like impalpable dust.

"Walt," Captain Jim McNelty, the famous Commander of the Border Battalion of the Texas Rangers, had said, "it seems hell's a-poppin' around the new oil strike town of Gunlock, which isn't overly surprising. An old shorthorn named Harper has been writing me letters asking for a troop of Rangers to quiet things down. As you know, and he oughta know, I haven't any troops to spare right now. So suppose you amble over there and quiet things down. If you figure it's too much for you or you get too bad scared, send me word and I'll come and lend you a hand."

Captain Jim meant it, despite his sixty-odd years and his hair as frosty as his temper. However, he did not fear that he would be obliged to take the long and hard ride to Gunlock, confident that his lieutenant and ace-man would soon have everything under control.

So Captain Jim sent Slade to a rendezvous with death.

That is, if both he and death kept their appointments.

2

Gunlock sat at the edge of the Cap Rock, that abrupt escarpment with a zone of broken country below called the breaks that bounds the western high plains on the east, its ragged crest often hundreds of feet above the mean level of the surrounding prairie. Not far north of the oil field was Sinking Creek, so called because after gushing from under a cliff of the northwestern hills and running for miles across the cattle and farm lands it dived into a hole in a ravine to pursue underground its course to the Rio Grande.

Sinking Creek supplied much of the water needed for John Harper's south pastures.

The railroad passed through Gunlock and then steel-stepped on to New Mexico.

El Halcón, with an appreciative eye for his turbulent surroundings, rode slowly down what passed for Gunlock's main street, and straight into trouble.

From the side door of a saloon dashed a man, a canvas sack in one hand, a gun in the other. He glanced wildly about, swerved onto the main street and halted directly in front of Shadow, Slade's magnificent black horse.

"Unfork! Gimme that cayuse!" he shouted and

15

lined his gun with the Ranger's broad breast.

It looked to the casual observer, like "the singingest man in the whole Southwest with the fastest gunhand" was caught settin'. He wasn't.

Slade's right hand moved like the flicker of a hummingbird's wing, too swift for the eye to follow. There was the crash of a shot. With a howl of pain, the gunman went backward heels over head to land in the dust of the street, writhing and moaning and clutching at his blood spouting shoulder.

A gun in each hand now, his eyes the color of frosted steel, Slade surveyed the suddenly silent crowd on the street over the rock-steady muzzles, one wisping smoke.

"Well, what's it all about?" he asked in pleasantly conversational tones.

From the front door of the saloon dashed a second man, blood streaming down his face.

"That's him!" he yelled, stabbing at the writhing figure on the ground with a finger. "That's the sidewinder! Larruped me with a gun barrel, grabbed the take and scooted out the door with it. I'll kill—"

"Hold it!" Slade interrupted, all the music gone from his voice. "Everything's under control. I guess that's your money in that sack. Call a doctor to patch up both of you. Then notify the town marshal, if you've got one, or the sheriff. Where can I find a livery stable?"

The saloon man stared, gulped. "Right around the next corner, to the left," he replied dazedly.

"Thank you," Slade said and rode on without a backward glance. Behind him a voice said in awed tones, "Good gosh all hemlock! Did you ever see such shootin'! That hellion had his gun on the big feller, but he might as well have left it in New Mexico for all the good it did him." He stared after Slade.

"Who in blazes is *he?*" he wondered.

"Dunno," replied the saloonkeeper, fingering his cut scalp. "But he's top man for my money. All right, some of you fellers, drag that horned toad to Doc Cooper's office. Hold onto him till the marshal gets there. I'll be along in a minute, soon as I stash away the *dinero*."

The wounded man, weak from shock and loss of blood and barely conscious, was jerked unceremoniously to his feet and, lurching and staggering, a captor's hand on each arm, led around a corner.

A few minutes later the saloonkeeper came out, a cloth wrapped about his head. However, he did not follow the others to the doctor's office but turned his steps to the livery stable he had recommended.

Meanwhile Slade had drawn rein before the stable door, which opened to his knock to reveal an elderly man who walked with a limp. He glanced at Slade, fixed his eye on Shadow.

"That's some critter!" he exclaimed. "Is he friendly?" he added dubiously as Shadow rolled his eyes and laid his ears back a little.

Slade liked the keeper's looks, so he replied, "If I tell him to be. It's okay, Shadow."

The old keeper chuckled understandingly and stretched forth a fearless hand, into which Shadow thrust his muzzle.

"I like a one man horse," the keeper said. "Had one once myself when I was following a cow's tail, before I got stove up in a stampede. He'll get the best and be right here when you want him." He nodded to a Sharpe's buffalo gun hanging from a peg as he spoke. Slade felt that Shadow would not be forced to take matters in his own hands, or teeth, rather, if somebody came in with notions.

"Say, didn't I hear a shootin' a minute ago?" asked the keeper as he began removing the rig. "Sounded close."

"Guess you did," Slade replied. The keeper glanced at him questioningly; but before *El Halcón* could elaborate, a knock sounded and a voice called, "You in there, Ben?"

"It's Chris Ames, who owns the Walking Beam saloon," said Ben, opening the door. "What the devil does he want?"

Another moment and he was staring at the saloonkeeper's bandaged head. "What in blazes—" he began.

Ames, without answering, turned to Slade and held out his hand.

"Feller," he said, "I didn't get a chance to thank you for what you did, but now I sure want to say much obliged; you saved me a heavy loss, besides givin' me a heap of satisfaction by downing that skunk. My name's Ames, Chris Ames; don't believe I caught your handle."

Slade supplied it and they shook.

"A darn good piece of work, only I wish you'd drilled the horned toad dead center instead of just bustin' his shoulder."

"Perhaps I would have had I known what it was all about," Slade replied. "I didn't, though, and figured a shoulder would slow him down a mite."

Ames's eyes widened. "You mean to say you picked the spot where you wanted to plug him, and him holdin' a gun on you?"

"I did," Slade said.

Ames shook his head. "Well, anyhow, you did a swell chore," he declared, "and I want to say much obliged again."

Slade's white even teeth flashed in a smile. "I really didn't have much choice in the matter," he deprecated. "The gentleman was acting like he meant business and I figured he'd better be stopped before he did something foolish."

"You stopped him, all right," Ames chuckled. "Reckon Doc Cooper is trying to put him together right now."

"Doc Cooper?" Slade repeated.

"That's right," nodded Ames. "We didn't have a doctor here till he showed up a couple of weeks back. He's old and sorta crusty, but he sure can stir his stumps when he needs to."

It was Slade's turn to nod agreement. As he well knew, old Doc Cooper was crusty, all right, and he could be plenty salty if necessary.

Not so surprising that he would show up in Gunlock. He was always on the move, and boom towns were his meat.

"Say!" exclaimed Ben, "what in blazes is this all about? What happened to your noggin, Chris?"

The saloonkeeper told him, vividly. Ben whistled, and eyed Slade with respect.

"Things like that happen often here?" the Ranger asked.

"Too darn often," growled Ames. "The town's a heller. Over close to the southwest field, which is the real tough section, a couple of places have been cleaned out. Men have been held up and robbed on the street in broad daylight. Several gents have been found in the morning with their pockets turned inside out and waiting comfortably in a dark corner for the undertaker. Oh, she's quite a town, but we're trying to tame things down a mite and get a local government going. Appointed a marshal last week and built a calaboose and hope to get a mayor 'fore long.

Yes, she's quite a town. New wells coming in all the time, and the railroad is building an assembly yard and putting up a roundhouse and a shop. We figure to be an oil center that'll make Beaumont and Port Arthur sit up and take notice before we finish."

"How did that fellow manage to catch you unawares?" Slade asked.

"Worked it mighty slick," Ames replied. "Slid in the side door—I could swear it was locked. I was just stuffing three days' take into the sack. I started to stand up, but he larruped me one and darn near knocked me out. Grabbed the sack and out the door he went. Guess I was a mite confused and I headed for the front door instead of following him. May have been a good thing that I didn't."

"Quite probably," Slade conceded. "*He* seemed a mite confused when he hit the street. Wonder why."

"I can tell you," said Ames. "Seems he left his cayuse tied at the end peg of the hitchrack. You know how cowhands get to figuring a certain peg belongs to them and don't like to have it took over by somebody. That peg has always belonged to Burns Morrow of the Lapped Circles spread. So when he found a critter there, he moved the critter down a few pegs and took the end peg. When the hellion run out he couldn't see his bronk where he left it. And tried to take

21

over yours; which was a mistake on his part."

"A darn painful mistake, I'd say," chuckled old Ben.

"Come on over to my place, Slade, and eat and drink on the house," Ames said. "Bring your pouches along; I got a nice room upstairs for you to sleep in. And Ben, the stable bill, whatever it is, is on me."

Slade started to demur, but Ames held up his hand. "Please," he said. "Please make me happy by letting me show my appreciation a mite."

"Very well, and thank you," Slade accepted. "First, though, I would suggest we visit Doc Cooper and let him take a look at your head."

"Just a scratch," Ames deprecated the injury.

"Maybe so, but then again maybe not," Slade differed. "I doubt if there is a fracture, but concussion that can't be detected by the layman may be present. You wouldn't know it yourself until all of a sudden you toppled over."

"Okay, guess you're right," Ames agreed. "Be seeing you, Ben."

Slade said so long to the keeper and followed Ames out the door. Old Ben gazed after him and remarked reflectively to Shadow—"Horse, you're just about the finest critter I ever saw on four legs, and the feller who forks you is just about the finest I ever saw on two. Yep, sure a fine looking man. Dresses like a chuckline ridin' cowhand, but I'll bet money he ain't. Wonder what he really is, and what he's doin' here? Well, reckon folks will find out 'fore long. Here's a double helpin' of oats for you; get on the outside of 'em."

Old Ben was right. Walt Slade was indeed a man whose appearance attracted more than a passing glance. Very tall, more than six feet, his wide shoulders and broad chest slimmed down to a lean, sinewy waist that matched his height. And his face was worthy of his splendid form. A rather wide mouth, grin-quirked at the corners, mitigated somewhat the tinge of fierceness evinced by the prominent hawk nose above and the lean, powerful jaw and chin beneath. His pushed-back "J.B." revealed a broad forehead and crisp, thick black hair.

The sternly handsome countenance was dominated by black-lashed eyes of very pale gray. Cold, reckless eyes that nevertheless usually seemed to have little devils of laughter dancing in their clear depths. Devils that, if occasion warranted, could be anything but laughing.

As Ben said, Slade wore the homely garb of the range—Levi's, the bibless overalls favored by the cowhand, soft blue shirt with vivid neckerchief looped at his sinewy throat, scuffed half-boots with softly tanned leather, and broad-brimmed rainshed—and wore it with the careless grace of a man who becomes his clothes, no matter what they are, not his clothes him.

About his waist were double cartridge belts, from the carefully worked cut-out holsters of which protruded the plain black butts of heavy guns.

And the observant might note that from those big Colts his slender, muscular hands were seldom far away.

He and Ames received stares a-plenty when they reached the crowded main street. Heads drew together in low-voiced conversation, but nobody intercepted them. In short order they reached the doctor's office.

The old frontier practitioner's eyes narrowed slightly as they rested on *El Halcón*, but he offered no comment.

"All right, let's have a look," he said to Ames. Deftly he removed the clean bar towel the saloonkeeper had wrapped around his head. His sensitive old fingers gently explored the vicinity of the wound.

"Nothing to it," was his verdict. "I'll cleanse and bandage it and you can go back to sellin' pizen to folks. You've got a skull like a cannon-ball—only a derrick walking beam could dent it." He crinkled his frosty old eyes at Slade, but still gave no sign that he recognized the "notorious" *El Halcón*. Slade grinned and said nothing. Very quickly, he knew, somebody else would recognize him as *El Halcón*.

Because of his habit of working undercover

whenever possible and often not revealing his Ranger connections, Walt Slade had acquired a peculiar dual reputation. Those who knew the truth, like Doc Cooper and the sheriff of this particular county, declared that he was not only the most fearless but the ablest of that illustrious body of law enforcement officers. Others, who knew him only as *El Halcón* of dubious activity with killings to his credit would just as vigorously maintain that he was nothing but a blasted owlhoot too smart to get caught, so far.

Which worried Captain Jim McNelty who more than once had expostulated with his lieutenant and urged him to do something to correct the erroneous impression.

"Sometime some trigger-happy deputy or marshal will take a shot at you, thinking he's doing the right thing," Captain Jim would say. "To say nothing of a professional gunslinger out to get a reputation by downing *El Halcón*, and not past shooting in the back to do it."

"But folks who know me as *El Halcón* will talk in a manner they never would to a known Ranger," Slade would reply. "And owlhoots who figure I'm just one of their brand sometimes get careless. And anyhow, if your number isn't up, nobody can put it up."

After which Captain Jim would grumble and Slade would laugh and go his carefree way as *El Halcón*, with no regrets for the past, content with the present, and giving scant thought to the future.

"The hellion you plugged?" Doc replied to Slade's question as to the whereabouts of the wounded robber. "Marshal locked him up. He wasn't feeling overly good, but he'll make out. Drilled high up, no bones busted. Unfortunately, that sort doesn't kill easy. Was still sorta dazed and couldn't talk sensible; just mumbled."

Slade nodded, and withheld his own opinion as to the fellow's inability to express himself coherently.

Ames chuckled when they reached the street. "A walkin' beam," he remarked. "That's what I named my place, 'cause in the beginning business went up and down just like a walkin' beam jigs. Place caught on, though, and I have nothing to complain about. I'd have had something to complain about if it hadn't been for you, though. Three days' take in that sack the hellion grabbed. More money than I would have liked to lose right now. Insured? Huh! They say Lloyds of London will insure anything, but I betcha they wouldn't insure a Gunlock business."

They turned a corner and Ames led the way to a second side door, which he unlocked.

"Right upstairs and stow away your pouches," he said. They mounted the stairs and Ames opened the door of a comfortable looking room.

"Here you are," he said, "and I hope you decide

to coil your twine in it for quite a spell. Here's a key, and one to the downstairs door. Be sure and lock 'em both when you come in. You saw what happened to me from leaving a door unlocked."

Slade nodded, but as anent the "voiceless" outlaw, he had his opinion as to that unlocked door. Locks didn't bother the kind of outlaw that was sifting into the section of late; more in the nature of an invitation, hinting as they did of something of value behind the bolt.

3

The Walking Beam was big, well-lighted, and spotlessly clean. The long gleaming bar with its blazing mirror, the roulette wheels, lunch counter, tables, and the polished dance-floor, at the moment unoccupied, were all comparatively new and in excellent condition. Chris Ames knew how to run a place, all right.

"First a snort out of my private bottle," said Ames as they approached the bar. He beckoned a waiter.

"Sam, take care of this gent," he directed. "Only the best for him, and everything on the house whenever he comes in."

Slade knew there was no use to protest the owner's generosity; Ames would only feel hurt. So he murmured a word of thanks and let it go at that.

"Take that table over in the corner by the dance-floor, so you can get a good look at the girls when they come on," said Ames as they raised their glasses. "I got some good lookers, and they're all square shooters, too; I won't have any other kind. Same goes for the games if you should hanker to take a hand at poker or something. I run a strictly square place, as everybody knows. That's why I'm doing the best business in town."

29

"It pays off," Slade agreed.

"So I found out long ago," Ames said, raising his glass. "Here's to more good shootin'."

Slade laughed and drank the toast with him. Then he repaired to the table and ordered a meal, leaving Ames to converse with his head bartender who eyed the Ranger with approval and respect.

While Slade was eating his dinner, the Mexican orchestra filed in, with the dance-floor girls following. Slade was willing to agree with Ames that there were some lookers among them, especially a couple of sloe-eyed little *señoritas*. They were a jolly bunch and all had a solicitous greeting for the injured owner. Undoubtedly Chris Ames was popular with the help, a good man to work for.

The Walking Beam was filling up with a cheerful and noisy crowd, for Gunlock's turbulent night life was already in full swing. Outside sounded the beat of hoofs as whooping cowboys raced their horses along the main street. The air quivered to a babble of voices and song, or what was apparently intended for it. The screech of locomotive whistles and the grinding of wheels provided a fitting undertone.

Slade eyed the colorful scene with appreciation and his pulse quickened. After a long and lonely ride, human companionship was welcome. He loved the rugged wastelands and from them he garnered peace, but a protracted spell of them with only his horse to commune with bred a desire for association with his fellows. After all, he was young, filled with lusty life, and he liked such surroundings. He leaned back comfortably in his chair with a cup of steaming coffee before him and rolled a cigarette with the slim fingers of his left hand.

Chris Ames came over to join him and his jovial countenance was graver than usual.

"Been doing some thinking," he announced. "Maybe that horned toad you plugged is just a lone wolf thief on his own, but maybe he might belong to the Cito Raiders."

"The Cito Raiders?"

"Uh-huh, that's what they call 'em 'cause they 'pear to hang out in the Cito Hills up to the northwest. They're the bunch that's been widelooping cows from the spreads to the north and east of here. They've held up and robbed a coupla stages and a bank or two. They're bad and nobody has been able to make any headway against 'em. I'd hate to see you get into trouble because of what you did for me."

"Don't let it bother you," Slade said. "And you really think that fellow might be one of the bunch?"

"I dunno," Ames replied frankly. "I just some-how got a feeling that maybe he might."

"Sounds interesting," Slade remarked.

"Too darn interesting," Ames growled. "As I

31

said, they're a bad bunch to go up against. Have a talk with the marshal and try and find out if he learned anything from that hellion. He said he'd be in later. And I expect Sheriff Blount Young will show up about tomorrow; he spends a lot of time here of late. I'll introduce you to him."

Slade smiled slightly but did not comment. Captain Jim had received a letter from Sheriff Young, in which the Cito Raiders were mentioned, unfavorably.

"Another snort?" asked Ames. "I'll send it over."

"I'll settle for another cup of coffee, if you don't mind," Slade replied.

"Anything you want," said Ames. "Try a whirl with one of the gals. That little curly-head named Dolores is something extra. I'll be seein' you— business is picking up."

He beckoned the waiter and hurried back to the far end of the bar.

The marshal did show up, a little later. Ames brought him over and performed the introductions. He shook hands warmly, accepted a chair and a drink.

"You did a good chore, son, a raunchin' good chore," he said. "A pity you didn't drill the devil about four inches lower down."

"Maybe better as is, if you can induce him to do a little talking," Slade replied.

"Could be," the marshal agreed. "So far,

though, I ain't been able to get him to say anything. Just grunts and mumbles and won't sit up. Not much wonder, though, I reckon. A forty-five slug packs a hefty wallop, no matter where it hits you. I'll try him again in the morning."

Slade nodded, his eyes thoughtful; he was recalling Doc Cooper's description of the wound—"high up, no bones busted." Seemed a bit unusual for a rugged individual to be prostrated by shock for so long a time.

The marshal chatted for a while, tossed off his drink, and stood up.

"Have to go out and amble around a bit," he said. "Something liable to start poppin' any minute. See you tomorrow."

Although he was a mite weary, Slade decided to take Ames's advice and try a whirl on the dance-floor. He singled out the big-eyed little *señorita*, Dolores, Ames mentioned, and requested her company for the next number. She agreed eagerly.

As they circled the outside of the floor, she murmured in Spanish, "I am so happy, *Cápitan*, that you chose me."

"Why?" he asked smilingly. She glanced about, then said, her voice very sweet and low, "Pablo, the orchestra leader knows you," she quoted softly, " '*El Halcón*, the just, the good, the compassionate, the friend of the lowly.' *Cápitan*, I am honored."

"It is I who am honored," he said soberly. "A man can aspire to no higher guerdon than the praise of a nice woman."

Her eyes laughed at him. "Dance-floor girls are not supposed to be nice," she giggled, adding, "But one must be nice does one hope to work for *Don* Christo; he will have no other kind.

"But he is not too strict," she said, with a roguish smile. "He likes for his girls to have nice friends; he says they work better if they do."

"*Don* Christo is a wise man," Slade chuckled. "One would do well to follow his advice."

"I think so, too," she agreed, glancing at him through her lashes.

"*Caro mio*," he said, "it's nearly midnight. We'll have one more number together and then I'm going upstairs to bed. Was in the saddle most of last night. I'll see you again tomorrow."

Her big eyes suddenly mirrored concern. "Lock well the door," she replied. "You may have made enemies today, and the evil love not *El Halcón*."

"I will," he promised, and meant it. He took her warning more seriously than he did Chris Ames's. Dance-floor girls, in their way, were wise and they didn't miss much. She might have overheard something she preferred not to mention at the moment.

In his room close to the stairhead, Slade shut and locked the door, leaving the key in the lock. He had little faith in that lock but he knew nobody could touch the door without awakening him. He partially undressed, laid his guns ready to hand, and stretched out on the bed. Almost instantly he was sound asleep.

Slade knew he could have been asleep little more than an hour when he was shot wide awake by a sound, a tiny screaking sound, as of metal rasping on metal; it came from the direction of the closed and locked door.

He whipped out of bed, deftly threw the blankets together to resemble a sleeping form, picked up his guns and glided silently across the room to the far wall, where he would be out of line with the light seeping in from the hall were the door opened.

Utterly motionless, he stood watching and waiting. The faint rasping sound ceased, was followed by the minutest of clicks, then the soft whisper of the turning knob. Slade's eyes never left the dim outline of the door.

In the direction of the door a thin line of radiance appeared, a mere sliver of light. Slowly, steadily it widened, inch by cautious inch, became a glowing bar, furry-edged with gloom.

There was something indescribably menacing in that slowly widening beam and the barely perceptible movement of the door. Slade could vision murder crouched with grim lip and curved back behind that stealthy movement, weapon in hand.

The beam ceased to widen, hung motionless, streaming across the simulated form on the bed. Slade tensed for action.

There was a moment of tingling suspense, then the room rocked to a blaze of gunfire. Bullets hammered the roll of blankets that twitched and jerked under the impact. Slade could just make out a shadowy something hugging the door jamb. He shot with both hands, left and right, again and again.

There was a whimpering cry followed by a crippled scuttering on the floor boards of the hall, then a thud, another and another, dimming downward. Slade bounded across the room for the door, peered out cautiously; the hall was empty.

Below, the monotonous murmur of the busy saloon had stilled. Now there rose a boom of voices. There was stirring in the occupied rooms along the hall. Slade whisked out the door and to the stairhead. Peering down he saw a huddled something at the foot of the stairs, close to the outer door that stood slightly ajar. He sped back into his room, closed and locked the door and slipped on a few clothes.

Now voices were bawling at the foot of the stairs. Another moment and somebody came pounding up the steps. Slade waited.

A knock sounded on the door, a hammering knock, and a voice crying something. Slade leisurely crossed to the door, unlocked and opened it to reveal the wild-eyed and scared face of Chris Ames.

"You—you all right?" the saloonkeeper gasped.

"Fine as frog hair," Slade replied. "Come in."

He drew the panting Ames into the room and closed and locked the door.

"You sure you're all right?" Ames repeated.

"Everything under control," Slade returned composedly. "Only I'm afraid your blankets over there will need a little patching; right now they're sorta airy."

"I knew damn well it was happening here," Ames gabbled. "Sounded like the war had started all over. I headed straight for your room, found the downstairs door open and fell over a carcass down there. What *did* happen?"

Slade told him, briefly. Ames swore with explosive violence.

"But how did the sidewinder get in?" he asked. "Didn't you have the door locked?"

"Yes, it was locked, with the key left purposely in the lock," Slade replied. "I knew nobody could jiggle that key without arousing me. The gentleman used a pair of thin, long-jawed pliers with which he was able to grip and turn the key and shoot the bolt. The same way that horned toad got into your back room yesterday, the chances are. A rather unusual procedure for this section, but times are changing, and so are men and methods."

"Well, anyhow you sure did for the skunk, shot to pieces," Ames growled. "I hear some of the boys coming upstairs, looking for me, I expect."

"Chris," Slade said, "will you do me a favor?"

"Couldn't very well refuse you anything, could I?" Ames returned. "What is it?"

"Keep what I told you under your hat," Slade replied. "May cause certain people to do a little puzzled guessing."

"Don't worry, the latigo's tight on my jaw," Ames assured him. "But what about the marshal, he'll be showing up any minute, if he ain't here already."

"Get him alone and tell him; he should know," Slade answered. "He's no blabbermouth, I'm willing to wager."

"He isn't," agreed Ames. "Old Hank Otey's all right. I'll take care of those blankets myself so nobody'll be talking about them, and wondering. We'll let the boys do some guessing, too. Okay, I'll see you tomorrow. What you going to do now?"

"I'm going to bed," Slade replied. Ames shook his head. "If it was me, I'd be settin' up all night with a gun in each hand," he declared. "Nothing seems to bother you. How you do it is beyond me."

Slade smiled, unlocked the door and let him out into the hall to face a babble of questions.

Although he had little fear of a repeat performance, Slade took the precaution to jamb a chair under the door knob before he turned in. Then he went to sleep again, not to awaken until past mid morning.

4

Ames had not yet arrived when Slade descended to the saloon, after shaving and cleaning up, and there was but a scattering of patrons present. So he enjoyed a leisurely breakfast and then relaxed comfortably with coffee and cigarettes to await developments.

They were not long in coming. Marshal Otey stalked through the swinging doors, and he appeared to be in anything but a good temper. He spotted Slade, waved a greeting, and joined him.

"Well," he said without preamble, "the gent you gunned yesterday is outa jail."

"Somebody bail him out?" Slade asked, although he knew very well that wasn't the case.

"Oh, sure, somebody 'bailed' him out, all right, but not in the usual and legal manner," Otey snorted. "I stopped at the calaboose for a look at him before I went to bed just before daylight. The door was standin' wide open and there wasn't anybody inside. How they got that door open is beyond me. Lock wasn't busted and I know darn well I locked it when I left yesterday evening."

"Duplicate key made from a wax impression, the chances are," Slade replied. "Appears somebody hereabouts is handy with locksmith tools."

"Too darn handy, and with other things, too,"

growled Otey. "Well anyhow, the scorpion you plugged last night won't be going anywhere, unless he manages to claw his way up through about four feet of earth."

"I've a notion he'll stay planted," Slade smiled. "You found those pliers I mentioned?"

"Yep, in his pocket."

For some moments the marshal was silent, sipping the drink a waiter brought him.

"Well," he said at length, "what do you think about it all?"

"First," Slade replied deliberately, "I think the gentleman you had locked up put on a very good act feigning semi-consciousness and inability to understand and answer questions. Secondly, that somebody was very anxious to make sure he wouldn't do any talking, which is interesting. Third, that he is, as doubtless the other was, a member of an efficient and well-organized outfit, quite likely with connections here in Gunlock, that is systematically plundering the section."

"My sentiments, now it's too late," grunted Otey. "You mean him and the other one belong to the Cito Raiders?"

"Not knowing who or what are the Cito Raiders, I would hesitate to say," Slade answered. "However, from what Chris Ames remarked about them yesterday, I consider it a possibility that should not be overlooked. What do you know about the Cito Raiders?"

"Not much," replied Otey. " 'pears they're a bunch that hang out in the Cito Hills and raid from there—that's how they got that loco name hung on them. You see, I ain't been marshal long and my authority holds good only in Gunlock. Tell you what, I figure Sheriff Young will show up here sometime today. I've a notion it would be a good idea for you to have a talk with him."

"I think so, too," Slade agreed.

"All of which sorta puts you on a hot spot, seeing that by no fault of your own you've got in bad with a bad bunch. Kinda hate to see you go, but it might be a good idea to trail your twine out of the section. Safer, anyhow."

"Nope, not yet," Slade replied carelessly. "My horse needs rest."

The marshal shot him an admiring glance.

"Don't scare easy, eh?"

"Not until I see something to be scared of," Slade smiled.

"Huh! I doubt if you've ever seen it," said Otey. "Or ever will," he added. "Well, guess I'd better go out and mosey around a spell. Here comes Ames. I'll give him the news first."

The saloonkeeper waved to them and went into conference with his head bartender. Otey approached him and they conversed earnestly for a few minutes, Ames shaking his head and glancing occasionally at Slade. After the marshal left he joined *El Halcón*.

43

"Had your breakfast yet?" he asked. "Okay, I'll order mine. Expect a big night tonight; payday for the oil workers and they'll all be out for a bust. Lots of cowhands always amble in then, too, and all the railroaders that aren't working the night shift. Things will really hum. How'd you and the marshal make out?"

"Okay," Slade replied. "I like him."

"He's a good Injun," said Ames. "You can depend on him in a tight spot."

Ames, with plenty to do, did not linger over his breakfast. "I took care of those blankets," he said as he rose to hurry back to the far end of the bar. "Dam lucky you weren't in 'em—they were full of holes. Some of the slugs stuck in the wall, but they ain't particular noticeable. Be seeing you."

After finishing his coffee, Slade decided to amble out and give the town a once-over. He quickly decided it was worth a look-see. Every establishment appeared to be doing a roaring business. Men stepped purposefully, their eyes bright. Gunlock was up and coming.

Gradually he worked his way to the southwest section of the town. He was ready to agree with Chris Ames that this was the really tough part of Gunlock. Here the many saloons, although comparatively new, were already acquiring a dingy look. Here were slouchy figures with furtive eyes, and slatternly women. The dregs of the community, always to be found in a boom town, gravitating to beneath the common level of the industrious citizens.

Reaching the outskirts of the town, he gazed over the horizon. To the northwest loomed the rugged Cito Hills. To the south and curving around to the east was the Cap Rock, a true wasteland, the naked rocks of its ragged crest gleaming in the afternoon sunlight.

Between the two ranges, Gunlock crouched like a bristly porcupine between two hungry wolves.

On all sides rose a veritable forest of derricks. Walking beams jigged their unceasing dance, raising and lowering the ponderous steel bits that churned their way through the stubborn earth to tap the seemingly inexhaustible treasures of Texas black gold that for untold ages had lain waiting. Waiting for the hand of man to raise it to the sunlight of which it was born.

Hoisting engines purred and sputtered. The clang of hammers, the rasp of saws, the scraping of shovels and the shouts of men quivered the air. Like ants the men swarmed over the land. Like ants their apparently unrelated activities forged onward to a common goal.

Texas black gold! That was changing the destiny of the Southwest empire, bringing wealth and prosperity to the many, arousing ruthless greed in some. A blessing and a curse. But with good prevailing at the last. Walt Slade felt he

45

was gazing into the pulsing heart of a nation. The nation it was his privilege to serve.

Skirting the town, he walked north toward where Sinking Creek, nearly a mile distant, danced and glittered in the sun. On the grass-grown bank he paused, gazing at the rippling water, a perplexed expression shadowing his face. On the placid surface was an undoubted oil slick, not very pronounced, but plainly apparent. It was the oil slick that caused old John Harper, owner of the big Walking H ranch, to curse Gunlock and declare the water was spoiled for cows and would very likely kill 'em if they drank it.

There were no derricks anywhere near, and the elevation of the creek bed was higher than that of the field. Slade's black brows drew together until the concentration furrow was deep between them, a sign that *El Halcón* was doing some hard thinking.

He raised his eyes to the Cito Hills and the level rangeland flowing eastward from their base, dropped them again to the purling stream, and shook his head.

Shortly before the death of his father, which had occurred after financial reverses that resulted in the loss of the elder Slade's ranch, young Walt had graduated from a famous college of engineering. He had planned to take a postgraduate course to round out his education and better fit him for the profession he had resolved to make his life's work. This, however, became impossible at the moment, so he was receptive when Captain Jim McNelty, with whom he had worked during summer vacations, suggested that he sign up with the Rangers and pursue his studies during spare time.

Long since he had gotten more from private study than he could have hoped for from post-grad courses and was eminently fitted to take up the pursuit of engineering. He had received more than one attractive offer of employment from certain high-placed individuals he had contacted.

Meanwhile, however, Ranger work had gotten a strong hold on him, providing as it did so many opportunities for doing good, for helping deserving people, and for serving the land he loved. Eventually he would become an engineer, but there was no hurry; he was young. He'd stick with the Rangers for a while.

Geology had always intrigued him and his knowledge of the science was exhaustive. So now he surveyed the terrain with the discerning eye of the geologist and engineer and gradually arrived at a certain momentous conclusion which he resolved to keep to himself, for a while at least. Sooner or later it might prove valuable, as his knowledge of engineering often had in the course of his Ranger activities. With a last look around, he turned and walked slowly back to Gunlock's bustling business section.

Arriving at the Walking Beam, he sat down and ordered coffee. He was sipping it when two men bulged through the swinging doors. One was Marshal Otey. The other was a big and massively built old gent with a mop of unruly grizzled hair, a drooping mustache, and keen blue eyes in a blocky face. Slade immediately recognized Blount Young, the sheriff of the county.

The pair made their way to Slade's table. Otey started to perform the introductions, but the sheriff interrupted him with, "Well, well! So the notorious outlaw is squattin' in our midst, eh? Otey, don't you know him?"

"Know him?" repeated the bewildered marshal.

"Uh-huh," said the sheriff. "There are plenty of folks who'll tell you he's just a blasted owlhoot too smart to get caught."

The marshal did not appear impressed. "There are always hellions who spread around loco yarns about decent folks," he replied.

"So!" chuckled the sheriff, as he dropped into a chair that creaked under his weight. "Done took you in tow, too, eh? He's good at that; for quite a while now I've been follerin' him around like a pet dog."

"Blount, will you tell me what the devil you're drivin' at with your terrapin-brained palaver?" demanded the exasperated Otey.

48

"Sit down, Hank," said the sheriff. "Sit down and have a look at *El Halcón*. Yep, that's him. Ever hear tell of him?"

The marshal had. He gazed, almost in awe, at the man whose exploits, some of them considered questionable in certain quarters, were fast becoming legendary throughout the Southwest.

Sheriff Blount shook with laughter. "How are you, Walt?" he said, extending his hand. "Good to see you again."

He cast a glance at the still slightly off-balance marshal. "Well, what do you think?" he asked.

"About the same as you do, I guess," Slade replied. "He's tight-lipped."

There was nobody nearby, so after the waiter had taken their orders and departed, from a cunningly concealed secret pocket in his broad leather belt Slade drew something which he held for Otey to see.

The dumbfounded marshal stared at the famous silver star set on a silver circle, the feared and honored badge of the Texas Rangers.

"Well, I'll—I'll be darned!" he sputtered. "*El Halcón* a Texas Ranger! Well, I'd oughta knowed it."

"Yes, undercover man for Captain McNelty," Slade said as he replaced the badge. "Now you understand why the pledge of secrecy."

"Yes, I understand," answered Otey. "Don't worry about me."

"We won't," said the sheriff. "By the way, how many has he killed since he landed here?"

"Why—why only one, I guess," replied Otey. "Busted another hellion's shoulder for him."

Sheriff Blount shook his big head in mock disapproval. "He's slippin'," he declared. "By this time he'd oughta 'counted for five or six.

"Now, Walt," he added in a more serious voice, "suppose you give me the low-down on things, if you don't mind."

In answer, Slade reviewed the recent happenings. The sheriff listened attentively in silence, tugging his mustache from time to time.

"It's a bad bunch," he commented when the Ranger paused. "Enough to give even *El Halcón* something to think about. They've sure raised the devil hereabouts of late, and nobody's able to do any good against them. What do you think?"

"For one thing, that they have connections here in Gunlock," Slade replied. "Connections that enable them to obtain needed information. For instance, I understand it was not generally known that the Medford stage they held up was carrying money, which it seldom does."

"That's right," agreed Blount. "The same goes for the Brinkley stage. Was supposed to be plumb secret that they were packin' *dinero*, but the hellions hit 'em at just the right time. Must have been a leak."

"Follows a familiar pattern," Slade observed.

"A tough and salty outfit with brains at the head. Different from the old brush-popping outfits and their hit-and-miss methods. A lot harder to run down."

"Wonder who is the he-wolf at the top?" Blount speculated.

"Hard to tell, but the chances are a lot of folks will be quite surprised when and if he is uncovered," Slade said. "That's part of the latter-day pattern, too."

"I wouldn't be surprised if old John Harper had something to do with the leaks," growled Otey. "He's a stockholder of the Medford bank and would know what's going on. He hates the town, and the railroad, too, and swears he's going to make trouble for both. He's a ringy old shorthorn. Wouldn't be surprised if he did let something slip."

Slade hardly thought so, having read the letters Harper wrote to Captain McNelty, but was forced to admit that hot anger sometimes causes men to do strange and unethical things.

"Who and what is Harper?" he asked.

There followed a very unflattering account of John Harper and his doings.

"Some folks here were hit mighty hard by those holdups," Otey concluded. "The money wasn't insured. Guess Harper was plumb pleased when he heard about it. He's been the big jigger of the section for quite a while, but the oil strike and the railroad sorta knocked him off his perch, and he don't like it. The farmers buyin' state land over to the east didn't set well with him, either. He says that land was always open range and shoulda stayed that way. He had quite a row with Bill Carr, his neighbor to the east, because Carr said the farmers had a perfect right to buy the land and settle on it. Carr's a sorta salty jigger himself and says what he thinks. He owns the C Bar C which ain't as big by a lot as Harper's Walkin' H but is a good holding, and Carr's a good cowman, a young feller but knows his business."

"I see," commented Slade, who had let the Marshal run on without interruption, feeling that the information he was imparting might prove to be of importance.

"Carr an old-timer here?" he asked. Otey shook his head.

"Nope, he came here not long before the oil strike. Inherited the spread from his uncle, old Preston Carr, who *was* an old-timer. Before he came here, Bill was a range boss for the XT up to the northeast. Went to school some, though, and he ain't anybody's fool. He brought some of the hands from up there and they're a plumb salty bunch. First rate cowmen, though."

"The XT is a big outfit," Slade commented. "A man must have something to be their range boss."

"So I figure," nodded Otey. "Bill Carr has a

lot of newfangled notions. He said that it's just a matter of time till there's barbed wire in this section and no open range which is more costly to operate, according to him. And that sure didn't set well with John Harper. And Harper's been kinda hintin' that Carr's herd is growing a mite faster than it should, and that maybe all the cows he's been losing don't go into the Cito Hills."

"He's got no business saying such things if he can't prove 'em," the sheriff broke in.

"I know he ain't," nodded Otey, "but Harper's an uppity old bird and I reckon he figures he can get away with anything. And after all, Carr is a newcomer here."

Slade nodded. He was developing an interest in Bill Carr.

"They been snappin' at each other for quite a while," concluded Otey. "Wouldn't be surprised if they end up in a real row if Harper don't come down off his high horse and leave Carr alone. Say! Talkin' of the devil! Here comes Carr right now."

5

Slade had already noticed the tall, broad-shouldered man with flashing black eyes, ruggedly good looking features, and an assured bearing who pushed his way through the swinging doors and headed for the bar. Capable, perhaps just a mite intolerant, and could be plenty hard did occasion warrant, was his diagnosis.

After Carr trailed three individuals in cowhand garb who also did not have the appearance of Sunday school teachers.

"Carr and some of his hands he brought down from the north," said Otey. "Reckon they're in for the payday bust, like everybody else. Be some more of 'em along later, I expect."

Cowhands from other spreads swaggered in. Now the oil workers, payday money burning holes in their pockets, streamed through the swinging doors, and other gentlemen Slade regarded with a dubious eye. The Walking Beam was beginning to hum. Soon the hum would louden to a rumble, a kaleidoscope of raucous sound. Yes, it was going to be a big night. The dealers at the gaming tables settled themselves in their chairs. The dance-floor girls would arrive early. Already the musicians were on the little raised platform which accommodated them and were tuning their instruments.

The never ceasing marvel of the wasteland's sunset flamed in the west. Strange and multi-colored fires played on the crests of the Cito Hills. The Cap Rock was a lava stream of molten bronze merging with the royal purple lower down. Overhead the stars would soon spangle the blue-black robe of the night, winking coyly to the lights of Gunlock that were beginning to twinkle amorous reply. A locomotive headlight beam cleaved the gloom to the accompaniment of booming exhaust, clanking siderods, and the crash of steel on steel. Slade felt his pulse quicken. Yes, it was going to be quite a night, with perhaps considerable excitement attendant. He noted and studied every man who pushed his way through the swinging doors. No telling who would show up before the hours of darkness were replaced by the rose and gold of the dawn.

"Well," said Otey, "I guess I'll go out and look things over."

"I'll go with you," said the sheriff. "Be seeing you, Walt, unless you want to come along." Slade shook his head.

"Not just yet," he replied.

Left alone, he settled himself comfortably in his chair with a cup of coffee. Later he would look things over outside. For the time being, however, he felt the Walking Beam could stand a little more attention.

The dance-floor girls came on. Little curly-haired Dolores waved to him. He returned the salutation and watched her dance away in the arms of a young cowboy who appeared quite enamoured of his pretty partner.

However, after a couple of numbers she left the dance-floor and joined Chris Ames at the end of the bar. They talked together for a few moments and then she began wandering slowly about the room, aimlessly it appeared, passing close to occupied tables, pausing now and then for a word with patrons she recognized. Finally she worked around to Slade's table.

"Hello, how are you?" she said in colloquial English. "Mind if I join you?"

Slade looked surprised as he drew out a chair for her.

"You spoke Spanish last night," he remarked.

"So that possible listening ears would be less likely to understand," she replied. "I'm a Texas girl. I was born in Texas, and so was my father. My mother was of Mexican descent."

"And the rest of your name?"

"It's Cameron," she answered, "Dolores Cameron."

Slade shook his head. "What a combination; Spanish and black Scotch! Fire under ice."

She shot him a glance through her lashes. "Fire melts ice—sometimes."

Slade chuckled. "Now I understand something

that had me wondering a bit." he observed. "Your hair."

"My hair?"

"Yes, it's quite curly, which is usually not the case with a Mexican girl."

"My father's hair was black and curly and his eyes were black," she said. "My mother's hair and eyes were also black."

"I see," he nodded. "How come you're working here?"

She shrugged daintily. "A girl must live," she replied. "And I like the work and it pays well, and Mr. Ames is a good man to work for. I was with him before he came here, when he owned a place in Fort Stockton. He brought me here with him, and several other girls."

Slade had ordered wine for her. She raised her glass to her lips and spoke over the rim, her voice suddenly lower.

"Those men at the corner table near the orchestra appear interested in you," she said. "They glance in your direction and as I passed I heard one say, 'Yes, that is him, all right.' I thought you should know."

"Thank you," Slade replied, his voice also low. "I'm glad you told me. So that's why you were ambling around."

"Yes. We floor girls hear and see things, when we wish to. I heard what happened last night and so I'm keeping my ears and eyes open. Mr. Ames approves."

"Nice to have someone look after me," he said.

"Remember the words I spoke in Spanish last night," she said. "As the Mexicans say, it is an honor to serve *El Halcón.*"

"That is complimentary," he answered. "But— impersonal."

Her dark lashes lowered, then raised.

"Impersonal?"

Just a single word, but it said more than would have a paragraph.

Suddenly her little hand clenched in a fist.

"I wish I'd been in my room, which is at the end of the hall, instead of on the floor," she said. "I have a gun, and I can shoot."

"I fear you are a dangerous woman," he chuckled.

"Not too dangerous," she said, her voice very soft and low.

"Perhaps not—with a gun," he returned pointedly.

She blushed and dimpled.

Slade had noticed the four men she mentioned, at the corner table, who now and then glanced toward him, but he had given them little thought. They were ordinary appearing individuals dressed in rangeland garb. He had noticed that one, a small man, wore two guns and that he had slender hands that lay perfectly still on the table top, something he considered significant. They were the kind of hands that, like his own, when they did move the movements would be sure, and swift.

"Guess I'd better be getting back to the floor; the customers will think I'm neglecting them," Dolores said. "Not enough girls to go around tonight, and the boys like to dance. Will you dance with me again, later?"

"I sure will," he promised. "After a bit I'm going out to browse around a little, but I'll be back."

"Please be careful," she said, and glanced toward the table occupied by the four men. Slade nodded.

"Here comes Mr. Craig Lane," she remarked, glancing toward the door. "I understand he represents a big oil dealer over east who is interested in the Gunlock output. Distinguished looking, don't you think? He talks with Mr. Ames."

Slade was inclined to agree with her. Craig Lane was tall, well formed, with straight features and tawny hair worn rather long. His dress was impeccable. He wore a long black coat, gray trousers, and shiny riding boots. A black string tie contrasted with the snow white of his ruffled shirt front. His broad-brimmed hat was black and neatly creased. Altogether, Slade thought, he gave the impression of being an able, adroit, and successful man of affairs.

"A fine looking gent, all right," he conceded. "Strikes me as the sort that would sweep a lady off her feet without much difficulty."

Dolores made a face at him. "You're not a girl," she replied pointedly.

"So I've been told," he admitted, crinkling his eyes at her. Dolores giggled, and glanced at him through her lashes.

"What's wrong with him?" Slade asked, apropos of Craig Lane.

"Oh, nothing that I know of," she replied. "Only he always seems to me the kind of a man who is in love with but one person in the world—himself. Which doesn't set well with a woman. Okay, I'll be seeing you after a while." She trotted back to the dance-floor.

Craig Lane had made his way to the far end of the bar and was conversing with Chris Ames. Slade dismissed him from his thoughts and again concentrated on the four men at the table, although not appearing to do so.

Of course they might merely have heard of the thwarted robbery of the day before and their curiosity was, not unnaturally, intrigued. Which might explain their apparent interest in him. But it might be otherwise. Dolores seemed suspicious of them, and he had learned not to disregard the opinions of dance-floor girls, especially where men were concerned.

Finishing his coffee, he was about ready to

depart when he observed Bill Carr, the C Bar C owner, make his way to the table occupied by the four men, draw up a chair and sit down, motioning a waiter to bring drinks. Heads drew together in conversation.

What was the meaning of this latest development, he wondered. Carr evidently knew the four men, and not just casually; his approach had evinced familiarity. Absently he noted that Craig Lane was leaving and that Ames was making his way across the room in his direction.

Ames sat down and beckoned a waiter.

"That feller who just went out is a big man," he said, jerking his thumb toward the swinging doors. "Name's Lane, Craig Lane. He represents Port Arthur oil interests and, I figure, is trying to corral a hefty part of the Gunlock output for them. Expect he's up against some competition, though. This strike is making folks set up and take notice. Seems to be a purty nice feller."

"Appears to be," Slade conceded, his eyes thoughtful.

"He knows I know a lot of the fellers who own wells," Ames continued. "I've a notion he figures I may be able to lend him a hand in working out his deals; asks a lot of questions."

While Slade and Ames were speaking, Bill Carr got up and moseyed back to the bar. His four table companions tossed off their drinks and sauntered out. Slade watched their progress to the door. They had apparently lost interest in him, for they did not again glance in his direction.

"Wonder who are those fellows Bill Carr was talking to," he remarked casually to Ames.

"Fellers he worked with up north," Ames replied. "They come down to sign on with him, he said. First time they've been in. Quiet bunch. Well, got to get back to work. This is going to be quite a night. You and little Dolores seem to make out okay, what?"

"We do," Slade agreed smilingly.

"A darn nice girl," said Ames. "I knew her folks well—they're both dead. Father died just about a year back. Dolores was sort of at loose ends. Her dad was okay but he never got on in the world. So I gave her a job in my place over at Fort Stockton and brought her with me when I came here. She's a big help with my book work and helps keep an eye on things. Likes the dance-floor—most gals who work on it do. Glad she took to you—reckon she could do a lot worse."

Slade smiled and did not comment.

She's more a pardner than employee," Ames confided as he stood up. "When she hands out some advice, I take it, knowing it's the best thing to do. Yep, she's okay."

With a smile and a nod, he headed back to the end of the bar. Slade waved to Dolores and sauntered out. Her eyes followed him a little anxiously.

6

Gunlock was wild, and getting wilder by the minute. The main street was crowded with rollicking oil workers out to make the most of the payday bust. Through the open doors of the saloons came the cheerful clang of gold pieces on the "mahogany," the click of bottle necks on glass rims, the whir of roulette wheels, the whining of fiddles, and the strumming of guitars. And always a roaring babble of voices.

A troop of cowboys raced their horses down the street, weaving in and out between pedestrians who cursed them, but jovially. It was payday and anything went.

They swerved around a corner. There followed a crackle of gunfire and raucous whoops. Slade chuckled. Young fellows letting off steam by peppering holes in the sky. Which was all right, just good clean fun. Except that it made things easier for anybody who might have off-color notions in mind; nobody would pay any mind to a stray shot or two.

Slade couldn't get Bill Carr's new riders out of his mind. And he was wondering a bit about them. The small man with the quiet hands who, unlike the other three, packed two guns, had the appearance, he thought, of the professional gunslinger.

Not that there was anything so remarkable about that. Carr, with conditions what they were in the section, might feel that he needed some hard shooting hands in his employ. Cowboys, as a rule, contrary to popular opinion, were not adept in the use of firearms. The really good shot and the quick-draw man were the exception in their ranks. Bowing to the prevailing custom, they carried guns, but seldom used them other than for making a noise or taking a potshot at a coyote or a rattlesnake, generally with no harm to either the little prairie wolf or the reptile.

Two guns almost always meant one of two things, a show-off or a real artist with the six-shooter. The trouble there being the difficulty of telling which was which, an error in judgment likely to be fraught with serious consequences for the individual making the mistake.

All of which *El Halcón* knew, and he didn't make mistakes. Just as he was pretty, sure he was not making one relative to the small man with the quiet hands.

And if Bill Carr really was bringing in some gunfighters, it might well mean that he anticipated a showdown with John Harper. And Slade certainly did not desire a range war on his hands to further complicate matters. Also, there was always the chance that such action on Carr's part might be otherwise motivated.

Well, he must hold his estimate of Carr and

Harper in abeyance until he learned more about them from personal observation.

Dismissing the two cattlemen from his thoughts for the time being, he strolled along, enjoying the turmoil and the various activities but in the meantime keeping a close watch on his surroundings. The gentleman of the night before, who contemplated snake-blooded murder and took the big jump in consequence, might have left friends with a hankering to even the score.

Also, Bill Carr's riders from the north had seemed to take an unusual interest in him, and what that might presage he had no way of knowing. So best not take chances.

Gradually he worked his way to the southwest portion of the town, where the lighting was poorer, the saloons more frequent and noisier. He was not wandering aimlessly but approached the section with a definite purpose in mind. If an attempt against him were going to be made, this was the logical place for it. And here, with the less crowded streets, it would be easier to guard against.

Confident that he could take care of himself, he rather hoped that an attempt would be made, for it might provide opportunity to get to the bottom of the condition that was plaguing the section, the condition he had been sent to remedy. He hadn't the slightest idea who were the Cito Raiders, so called, or where they hung out. He was sure that in Gunlock or its environs was somebody who was the guiding genius of the outfit, who gleaned information that enabled the bunch to stage their operations with precision and profit. He had encountered similar conditions, products of the new brand of outlawry coming into being. And somewhere in this maze of twisted streets and ramshackle buildings might be the real headquarters of the band. They doubtless had a hidden hideout somewhere in which they could lie low for a while when it was expedient to do so, but he believed the real base of operations was in the town. He strolled on, watchful and alert.

Now the streets were becoming narrower, the lighting even less adequate. Voices were more raucous, the laughter of women taking on a shriller note. It seemed to Slade's vivid imagination that here arose a noxious effluvium of evil, an emanation invisible but very real. Here was the very bottom of the pit of sinister influences to be found in all such towns as Gunlock. He continued his slow stroll.

Suddenly he tensed. From the shadows ahead, two furtive figures had appeared, headed in his direction. However, before they drew near, they slid around a corner into a side street. Slade was pretty sure they cast swift glances in his direction before vanishing from his sight.

With caution, he approached the corner. When

he reached it and peered cautiously around a building wall, one of the few street lights at the far corner, no great distance away, showed it empty. He walked on.

Then from around a second corner, perhaps twenty yards distant a man swerved at a fast pace, glancing over his shoulder as he ran in Slade's direction.

Another instant and a second man bulged into view, shouting curses. A score of feet from where Slade had halted, the first man whirled to face the second. Both jerked guns and began blazing away as Slade instinctively slewed sideways against the building wall.

A bullet fanned the weaving Ranger's face. A second chipped the wall scant inches from his head. Now the first man had spun around. The second surged forward to join him.

And *El Halcón* understood.

Ducking, slewing, swerving, Slade drew and shot with both hands. The foremost man pitched forward to lie motionless. The other lined sights with the Ranger's breast—and died, two bullets laced through his heart. Slade whirled and sped back the way he had come, for a dozen yards. He halted, turned and, holstering his guns, strolled forward again.

A nice try, with an original touch. What appeared to be a corpse and cartridge session between the two was in reality an attempt at

69

snake-blooded murder. The second man had fired over his "adversary's" shoulder, not *at* him, and only *El Halcón*'s marvelous coordination of mind and muscle had saved him from catching the slug dead center. Yes, a very nice try, only, it didn't work!

Heads were popping out doors, a crowd gathering around the two bodies. A man in a white apron turned as Slade drew near.

"Did you see it, feller?" he called.

"Guess I did," *El Halcón* replied.

"What happened?"

"One of those gents bulged around the corner down there, the other behind him," Slade replied. "They stopped and began throwing lead."

Which he considered enough of an explanation.

The aproned man shook his head and clucked in his throat.

"Well, they sure did a first rate chore on each other," he said. "Both dead as doornails. Come along to my place—just a few doors down— and have a drink. I've sent for the marshal and I expect he'll like to ask you a question or two about what happened, seeing as you 'pear to be the only eye-witness.

"That is if you don't mind going up against him," he added with a grin.

Not in the least," Slade smiled. He liked the fellow's jovial face and ready grin and decided to accept the invitation, might work to his advantage to do so. A single glance had told him that neither of the killers belonged to the quartet of Bill Carr's new hands who appeared to take an interest in him at the Walking Beam. The saloonkeeper chuckled.

"I asked because some of the boys down here are sorta leary about coming to close quarters with the law," he explained. "Scairt he might recognize 'em next time, or something, I reckon. Oh, they're not too bad, but now and then they do things really nice folks sorta look sideways at.

Here's the Buzzard Bait," he added as they entered a saloon Slade didn't think too bad. He waved his hand to the bottle-pyramided bar.

"We got plenty of buzzard bait," was his explanation for the somewhat unusual designation of his place, and he chuckled still again.

The crowd was filtering back in, perhaps not wishing to be too close to the bodies when the marshal arrived.

The saloonkeeper bustled behind the bar and carefully chose a bottle, not from the pyramids but from under the bar.

"My own pizen," he chuckled as he filled two glasses to the brim. Slade sampled his glass and decided that the Buzzard Bait owner was a connoisseur of good whiskey.

"My name's Evans, Bob Evans," the saloonkeeper offered. "Don't think I caught your handle."

Slade supplied it and they shook hands.

Evans' brow wrinkled. "Slade," he repeated. "Seems to me I've heard that name."

Abruptly his face brightened and his infectious grin flashed out.

"Feller, I've got you spotted," he said. "You're the young feller who kept Chris Ames from getting robbed. Give me that paw again!"

He shook hands a second time, warmly. "Chris is a mighty fine feller," he said. "A mighty good friend of mine. Fact is, he helped me open this joint; I didn't have quite enough money of my own to swing it. I'm sure glad to know you. Just a minute, please." He hurried off to lend the busy bartenders a hand.

Conjectures as to what caused the shooting were flying back and forth. The general consensus appeared to be that it was a disagreement over cards, or a woman, or something equally unimportant.

Sipping from his glass, Slade studied the boys. He was inclined to agree with Evans. Quite likely there were some scalawags among them, but they didn't look too bad. Certainly not of the calibre of the pair lying on the sidewalk up the street.

Suddenly the babble of talk stilled. Glancing toward the swinging doors, Slade understood the reason; Marshal Otey had just stalked in and was regarding the gathering with frankly disapproving eyes.

The eyes widened as they rested on Slade. "Well, I'll be darned!" he growled.

"Come and have a drink, Hank," the Ranger invited.

"Don't mind if I do," the marshal accepted. "What happened down here, do you know?"

Slade repeated the exact explanation he had given Evans. Otey nodded and looked decidedly skeptical.

"Evans, did anybody recognize those two hellions?" he asked. The saloonkeeper shook his head.

"If they did, they didn't admit it."

"They wouldn't," snorted the marshal. "Well, I guess the world didn't lose much."

"I'll have some of the boys get shutters and pack the carcasses to your office," Evans offered.

"That'll help," accepted the marshal. "Much obliged, Bob."

Evans rattled off a string of names. Half a dozen men trooped out to handle the chore.

Otey polished off his drink and turned to Slade. "Ready to amble back up town?" he asked.

"Guess we might as well," *El Halcón* agreed.

"Come again, Mr. Slade," Evans begged. "We can't always promise such entertainment—"

"Oh, no?" the marshal interrupted.

"But we'll do the best we can," Evans concluded, with his youthful grin.

Outside, Otey said, "Well, just what did happen?"

Slade told him, in detail. The marshal swore pungently.

"After you hot and heavy, eh?" he remarked.

"Sort of that way," Slade conceded. "If they keep on, perhaps they'll make a bad mistake and give me something to work on."

"A nice prospect, I must say," snorted Otey. "Two tries in two nights is going a mite strong."

"Neither worked, and that's what counts," Slade replied cheerfully. "Suppose we stop at your office and give those two gents a look. They might be packing something of interest, although it's not likely; their kind seldom does. Can't always tell for sure, though; best not to overlook any bets."

Slade was right in his surmise. The bodies divulged nothing of significance save, as the marshal said, "Just like the other hellion you plugged last night, packin' a lot more money than their sort have any business to be packin'. Hellions have been doing all right by themselves. What shall we do with it?"

"Stow it away," Slade answered. "You'll find use for it once you get your town government going."

"That's an idea," agreed the marshal as he pocketed the *dinero*.

The two men were ordinary looking customers,

74

with nothing to differentiate them from the average range rider, except that their hands showed no recent marks of rope or branding iron.

"The taller one once worked as a cowhand, but I'd say the other never did," Slade decided. "Which is interesting."

He examined the smaller man's linty pocket seams with care, rubbing his fingers along the edges and scrutinizing the results, his eyes thoughtful.

"Well, put them on exhibition," he said. "Perhaps somebody may recall them and possibly whom they were with. Well, I guess that's all we can do here."

"So let's toddle over to the Walking Beam for a snort and maybe a bite to eat," suggested the marshal.

"That Bob Evans who owns the Buzzard Bait is all right," he remarked as he locked the office door. "I thought maybe he was wrong in locating where he did, but maybe he knew what he was doing."

"He did," Slade replied. "That section will be cleaned up after a while and it's closer to the field than any other portion of the town. He should do a good business that will keep getting better as the town grows."

"That's what he told Chris Ames, who helped him get located," the marshal said.

7

At the Walking Beam, Otey ordered a surrounding which he put away with gusto. Slade settled for coffee and a cigarette. After waving a greeting to Dolores, he gave himself over to some very serious thought.

The attempt on his life denoted, he felt, ingenuity well above the average. No clumsy method such as trying to drygulch him from an alley mouth, which somebody acquainted with *El Halcón* evidently figured, rightly, would not work. Whereas the mock street fight staged by the two killers would be calculated to throw the victim off balance for the moment needed to do away with him. And, Slade was forced to admit, it came close to being successful. His habitual vigilance and his instinctive move to get out of the line of fire had proved the killers' undoing. At that distance the chance of *El Halcón* not getting in the first deadly shot was negligible. When the bullet the killer fired over his companion's shoulder missed its mark, he had about as much chance as a rabbit in a houn' dog's mouth.

The try the night before had also been well planned and executed, and would have probably succeeded against anybody who lacked Walt Slade's extraordinarily keen hearing and his uncanny ability to instantly diagnose an unusual sound.

So, everything considered, it was evident that he was up against a dangerous and resourceful bunch with somebody with plenty of brains directing the operations.

Who? Slade hadn't the slightest notion, so far. Bill Carr looked like a possible, even obvious suspect. A bit too obvious, Slade thought, having learned to distrust the obvious, but he could be wrong. Carr was a newcomer to the section, about whom nobody seemed to know much, and who had quickly succeeded in arousing the antagonism of old-timer owners.

All of which might mean nothing, but could be important. So far, he did not really list Bill Carr as a suspect but considered him worthy of some attention.

The C Bar C owner was still drinking and conversing with his men, who appeared to keep largely to themselves. While the marshal ate, Slade studied Carr.

Aggressive to the verge of being belligerent, he concluded. A hard man, all right, but not necessarily a bad one. One had to be hard to be range boss for the great XT spread in the northern panhandle, an outfit not noted for sweetness and light. That Carr had really been range boss for the XT he did not doubt. The ranch was too well known for such a claim to be falsely made.

Sooner or later somebody would be sure to uncover the deception. He put Carr in the back of his mind for further consideration and turned his attention elsewhere. It soon centered on Dolores, who again was wandering about the room in her apparently aimless manner. He wondered if the little dance-floor girl had heard something else she considered significant.

Well, if she had, he'd undoubtedly hear about it. Every now and then she cast a glance in his direction and smiled. She was a cute little thing, all right, and had plenty under her curly black hair.

Carr's four new hands filed in. He beckoned them and they joined him at the bar. Slade noted that the eyes of the quiet little man who wore two guns were constantly roving about the room. His belief was strengthened that the fellow was or had been a professional gunslinger, no doubt with his gun for hire. He put *that* in the back of his mind for future reference, too.

"Here comes Blount Young," Otey suddenly announced. "Reckon he's been looking things over."

The sheriff paused at their table and drew up a chair. A waiter hurried to fill his order. He regarded Slade severely.

"Why did you have to go prowling those rum holes down by the field?" he demanded. "Don't you know that was just asking for trouble?"

"Well, I wasn't sent here to just pick daisies and sample Chris Ames's whiskey," Slade replied smilingly. "And down there, I figured, should be productive of results; it was." The sheriff snorted.

"Too darn productive, I'd say," he grumbled, and was silent.

A few minutes later, Bill Carr left his companions and sauntered to the table, glancing questioningly at Slade. Marshal Otey performed the introductions.

Carr shook hands with a good grip, shot a second glance at Slade and smiled slightly. Slade knew very well that Carr had recognized him as *El Halcón*. However, the rancher proffered no comment and accepted the invitation to sit down and have a drink. He turned to Sheriff Young.

"Sheriff," he said, "there's something I have up to the moment hesitated to mention to you for fear of being misunderstood. I don't want you to think I'm just taking a dig at John Harper because of the things he's been saying about me, but I've made up my mind that I should no longer refrain from telling you."

"Well, what is it?" asked Young.

"Just this," Carr replied, "I've been losing cows of late."

"That so?" the sheriff countered. "Where they been run to? Do you know?"

"I presume that you mean in what *direction* have they been driven," Carr replied. "Well, the

Cito Hills are to the northwest of my holding, I believe."

"Which means, I gather, that *you* mean they'd have to cross the Walking H holding to get to the hills," retorted Young. "Are you levellin' a charge of cow stealin' at John Harper?"

"I'm not levelling anything at anybody," Carr answered quietly. "I'm merely stating the facts as they stand; you can draw your own conclusions."

"My conclusions are that you and John Harper are both plumb loco for hinting, both of you, that the other has been wideloopin' or helping to wideloop your cows," the sheriff stated flatly. "If either one of you can come up with some proof that the other has been pullin' a mite of cow stealing, I'll act. Oh, sure, if you've been losing stock it means the critters would have to cross Harper's holding to get to the hills, but that doesn't mean Harper had anything to do with it. His holding is a big one and it wouldn't be impossible for the hellions to run a herd across at night without him knowing anything about it."

"Granted," Carr agreed. "As I said, I'm not accusing anybody of anything. I merely tell you that I've been losing stock, and I figure it is your business, as a law enforcement officer, to try and do something about it."

He glanced at Slade, and again he smiled

slightly. *El Halcón* felt that Carr's talk was directed not at the sheriff but at himself. Why? As to that he was not at all sure, yet.

"Up in the panhandle," Carr observed reflectively, "we had to take the law in our own hands; we got results."

Sheriff Blount bristled. "I'll not stand for anything like that here," he declared. "I'm serving notice on you, Carr, and I intend to serve it on Harper."

Carr shrugged. "What do you think about it, Mr. Slade?" he asked abruptly.

"I think," the Ranger replied quietly, "that when honest men disagree and begin blaming one another for everything off-color that happens in a section they are letting down the corral bars and inviting the outlaw element to walk in."

As he spoke, he let his glance travel across the room and rest squarely on the small and quiet two-gun man who leaned against the bar, his gaze fixed on the occupants of the table, almost as if he were taking part in the conversation. From the corner of his eye he noted that Carr flushed a little, but when he spoke his voice was composed and sober.

"You may have something there," he conceded. "I've a notion you should know."

Which latter statement, Slade felt, was decidedly ambiguous. He was swiftly becoming convinced that Bill Carr, no matter what else he might be or might not be, was a shrewd article who didn't miss many bets.

Carr ordered drinks for the sheriff and Otey and coffee for Slade and returned to the bar, where he engaged the little two-gun man in conversation.

"I'm darned if I can make that young hellion out," the sheriff complained querulously. "He sounded like he was telling the truth when he said he was losing cows. Well, he's a small owner and can't afford to lose too many."

"And Harper?" Slade asked.

"Oh, old John is a big owner, all right, but I happen to know he's mortgaged up to the hilt," the sheriff replied. "A while back he did one of those foolish things even a smart *hombre* will do at times. He bought the Morton place up to the north of his range, a good piece of property but which he didn't really need, and borrowed the money to do it with from the Medford bank with his holdings as security. Note payments fall due before very long, I understand. So he can't afford to lose too many, either."

"Meaning that if he can't meet the note when it falls due, the bank might refuse to grant an extension?" Slade asked.

"I've a notion that's just about the case," Young replied. "The bank has a lot of land paper out and I understand the directors and stockholders are beginning to ask a question or two. A bank can over-extend itself, too."

"So it's possible Harper could lose his ranch," Slade commented.

"That's about the way it stands, I guess," the sheriff admitted.

"I see," Slade said, his eyes thoughtful. He was thinking of the walk he took to the banks of Sinking Creek, from where he had studied the geological formations to the north and west. He was beginning to see, vaguely as yet, the motive.

Otey glanced at the clock. "Well, reckon I'd better make another round," he said. "Seems peaceful enough in here for all the racket the hellions are making."

"I'll go with you," said the sheriff, "and if we can manage to keep Slade inside, maybe the rest of the night will pass without something bustin' loose."

"I'll try and stay inside," the Ranger promised, with a smile.

With Dolores heading for the table as the sheriff and marshal stood up, he felt there was a very good chance that he would stay inside till closing time. Indeed, he decided to do so, did nothing happen to force him to alter his decision.

Another moment and she was in the chair beside him. I waited until you were alone," she stated the obvious, with a glance at him through the dark lashes that always gave him the impression of shadow-tracings against her soft

84

cheeks. His resolve to remain in the Walking Beam was strengthened.

"Something to tell me?" he asked.

"I believe so," she replied. "I overheard the little man talking with Mr. Carr say something that puzzled me. He spoke very low, but I have good ears and I caught it. He said, 'With him here, anything can happen.' What he meant I don't know, but I am sure he was referring to you. I think he knows you."

"He probably does, as *El Halcón*," Slade conceded. He wondered just what the fellow did mean by the seemingly cryptic remark.

"Thanks for telling me," he said. "You're a help. Now don't say it is a privilege to serve—"

She interrupted his banter, "A privilege and a pleasure to serve—*you!*"

"I trust and hope you'll always find it so," he said.

"You'll find out," she answered gaily, smiling and dimpling. "Look, there comes Mr. Lane again; he looks mad about something."

Slade thought, too, that the oil buyer appeared to be in a bad temper. He scowled, glanced about the room. This time he did not approach Chris Ames, but turned to the bar and ordered a drink, which he consumed with dispatch. A second followed the first, after which he walked out, still frowning. Slade thought that he was probably having trouble closing his deals for the Gunlock output; the competition for the product of the growing field might well be stiff.

"I've some paper work in the back room to do for Mr. Ames," Dolores said. "No, I'm not going on the floor again tonight. Anyhow, it's getting quite late and things are quieting down."

Things were, for tired nature was taking toll and, after all, the celebrants had worked hard all day, most of them, and there would be more work to do the next. Bill Carr and his hands departed, the rancher waving goodnight to Slade, who concluded there was nothing more to be learned in the Walking Beam.

A little later, Dolores reappeared. "I'm finished," she announced.

"So am I," Slade replied.

Old Chris Ames smiled and looked pleased as they left the saloon together.

8

When Slade descended to the Walking Beam around noon for some breakfast, he found Sheriff Blount Young already present. With him was a big old gent with grizzled hair and a bad-tempered expression.

"Walt," said the sheriff, "I want you to know John Harper, who owns the Walking H spread. John, this is Walt Slade, the young feller I was telling you about."

"So!" rumbled Harper as they shook hands. "So you're the feller who's been making some headway against the horned toads squattin' here-abouts."

"Not too much, I fear," Slade replied smilingly as he sat down.

"More than anybody else has been able to do," said Harper, with a pointed glance at the sheriff. "Well, what do you think of the situation here?"

"Among other things, that there is altogether too much loose talk being bandied about."

"You do, eh?" growled Harper. "Just what do you mean by that?"

"Take your own case, for instance," Slade replied. "Casting aspersions at your neighbors, hinting at what you cannot prove is not commend-able in a man of your stature in the community."

Old John evidently understood perfectly what Slade was referring to.

"I never said the young hellion was stealin' my cows!" he bawled.

"Would have been better if you'd come right out and said it," Slade retorted. "Better than resorting to innuendo and snide remarks. If you openly accused Bill Carr, he would have a comeback, legal or otherwise."

Old John swelled like a bullfrog taking a deep breath, but the cold, pale eyes boring into his stemmed what appeared to be a coming volcanic explosion.

"I ain't used to having folks talking to me that way," he said thickly.

"Getting used to it may do you some good," Slade snapped.

"John," the sheriff broke in, "didn't I tell you not to tangle with him, that he'd take your hide off. Last night, he set Carr back on his heels the same way. Want to know why? Because he's always got the truth on his side and can back up what he says."

John Harper glared. Then he did a surprising thing—he grinned. And abruptly his bad-tempered old face seemed wonderfully pleasing and youthful.

"Blount," he said, "I've a notion you've got the straight of it." He turned to Slade.

"Much obliged, son," he chuckled. "Guess I

have been making a mite too much big medicine. I'll tighten the latigo on my jaw. Here's my hand on it."

He thrust forth his big paw again, and Walt Slade smiled, the flashing white smile of *El Halcón* that men, and women, found irresistible.

Later, when they were alone, old John confided to the sheriff, "Blount, when he smiled at me it made me feel good all over—sorta warm. As if I'd just passed some sort of hard test. I never saw such a pair of eyes as he's got. They seemed to look right inside of me and see what was there. And all of a sudden I was plumb scared they'd find something they didn't think well of. And when he smiled they changed. Was just like the sun all of a sudden breaking through a cold, gray cloud."

"Yes, he affects most everybody that way," said the sheriff. "A strange feller, but a man to ride the river with."

John Harper nodded sober agreement to the highest compliment the rangeland can pay.

At the table, old John bellowed for a waiter. "Bring us a snort and then we'll eat," he said. "Make mine a double order of hog hip and cackle berries. I crave nourishment."

They enjoyed a very pleasant breakfast together. After he had put away his double order of ham and eggs, Harper said, "Well, I'll have to be getting back to the spread and see what else has busted loose.

"Ride out and see me soon," he told Slade. "You can't miss my place. Just follow the north trail. First house you come to—big white *casa* on the right side of the trail."

"I'll do that, Mr. Harper, and very shortly," *El Halcón* accepted the invitation.

After the rancher had departed, Sheriff Young said to Slade, "He didn't mention what he rode in to see me about, but last night he lost more cows, between seventy and eighty head. I thought it funny last night when none of his hands were in town for the payday bust. John figured he'd try and put one over on the thieves. He figured with everybody in town for the bust they'd make a try for another herd. So his boys headed for town sorta late, but before it got dark, when anybody keeping tabs on them could see. But soon as it got dark, they turned around and skalley-hooted to the hills. They strung out all along the base of those rises. It was bright moonlight before nine o'clock and they swore nobody could have passed into the hills without their seeing 'em; but somebody did. And drove nigh onto eighty head of cows into them. Lank Jim Sanborn, Harper's range boss, is fit to be tied. Threatened to quit, and he's been with Harper nigh onto twenty years, when John sorta intimated there might be something wrong with his eyesight."

"I see," Slade said. He gazed out the window toward those rugged and mysterious hills that held their secrets well; but his eyes seemed to pass over them and look into the far distances.

"Blount, I'm going to take a walk," he said abruptly. The sheriff gazed at him and nodded, asking no questions. He had learned to respect those abstracted silences, knowing that *El Halcón* was pondering something which he would reveal in his own good time and not before.

Slade did take a walk, to the south bank of Sinking Creek, where once again he stood studying the terrain. For a long time he gazed at the Cito Hills that seemed to leer at him, derisively. Back and forth his eyes swept the immediate terrain, centered on the oil-slicked surface of the stream.

Yes, the oil slick was still there, still slight, but definite. He turned and glanced toward the ominous loom of the Cap Rock to the south, studied the forest of derricks that marked the Gunlock oil field, turned once more to follow the course of Sinking Creek with his eyes.

"I'll bet my last peso I'm right," he muttered to himself. "Yes, right both ways; all I have to do is prove my deductions to the satisfaction of others."

He walked slowly back to the town and its boom and bustle. Sooner or later it would be a good town, with peace and prosperity for all. Worth striving to bring those conditions about.

His thoughts turned back to John Harper's

widelooped cows. Obviously, according to Harper's account, they had been run into the Cito Hills. *Obviously!*

Again the obvious, in which *El Halcón* had learned to put little faith, or to at least view with a certain skepticism. Stolen cows had always been driven into the Cito Hills and the New Mexico markets, so of course they always would be.

Such was the accepted local viewpoint. Walt Slade was beginning to wonder.

Gradually he worked his way to the southwest portion of the town, where he entered the Buzzard Bait. Bob Evans, the owner, was present and greeted him warmly.

"Things were quiet the rest of the night, after you and Otey left," said Evans. "That shooting seemed to sorta sober the boys a bit. Anyhow they were plumb peaceful and behaved themselves better than ordinary. For which I was darned thankful; the less trouble the better."

Slade agreed with Evans, had a drink with him, then left the saloon and walked to the fields, where everything seemed to be hectic confusion but was in reality efficient order.

For quite a while he studied the operations, his thoughts dwelling on the pocket seams of the smaller of the two killers who had attempted to drygulch him the night before.

For in those linty seams was a caking of oily grit, evidence that the fellow had spent a good deal of time in the vicinity of the field, had very probably worked there. Which was, he felt, worthy of some thought. If the fellow was a member of the Cito Raiders, it hinted at rather surprisingly varied interests on the part of the outlaw band.

Well, the field was an excellent place to pick up information relative to local activities. Perhaps he had been planted there for just that purpose. Which would possibly explain the unexpected robberies of the two stagecoaches that were packing money at that particular time, contrary to their usual custom.

Suddenly he saw a man approaching who looked familiar. Another moment and he recognized Craig Lane, the representative of Port Arthur oil buying interests, or so he said. Lane waved a greeting.

"Mr. Slade, is it not?" he said. "Chris Ames pointed you out to me the other night and told me how you saved him from being robbed. An excellent chore on your part. Ames is a fine fellow and I would have hated to have him suffer a misfortune. I saw you last night in the Walking Beam and very nearly stopped to say hello. But I was kinda out of sorts because of something that had happened earlier in the evening and wasn't good company for even myself," he added with a grin.

He held out his hand and shook with a firm

grip. "Looking things over, eh?" he remarked. "All this must seem strange to a cattleman. Come along and I'll explain things."

Slade was agreeable and they walked on together, Lane pointing out things of interest, waving his hand now and then to somebody he recognized.

He showed, Slade thought, an exhaustive and accurate knowledge of oil well drilling and attendant activities.

They neared a derrick which was in the course of construction. On a platform some thirty feet above rested a stack of big squared timbers, back of which two men appeared busy.

Lane had slowed a moment to roll a cigarette and *El Halcón* was a pace or two in front of him.

Slade had almost reached the derrick when his keen ears caught a slight creaking sound overhead. He glanced up and bounded forward as a shadowy something rushed down toward him.

At his very heels, one of the ponderous timbers hit the ground with terrific force. Had it struck him, it would have crushed his skull like an eggshell.

Lane let out a roar of anger. "What the blankety-blank blue blazes are you trying to do, kill somebody?" he bawled. "That thing just missed us!"

"Sorry, sir!" a voice replied from above. "It got away from us."

"Yes, I guess it did," Lane answered sarcastically. "Come on and let's get out of here before something else happens," he said to Slade. "No wonder they have so many accidents down here—just plain carelessness."

"Accidents will happen, and no damage was done," Slade replied cheerfully. Lane growled and muttered, his anger apparently not appeased.

They walked on, Slade in silence, Lane still fuming over the confounded carelessness. Reaching the edge of the field, he paused.

"I'll have to leave you here, have an appointment," he said. "Perhaps I'll see you in the Walking Beam tonight, if you happen to be there."

"Chances are I will be," Slade replied. "Be seeing you, and thank you for everything."

"You came near having to thank me for getting your head busted open," Lane said morosely. "I should have been more on the lookout, being familiar with conditions here."

With a wave of his hand he hurried off. Slade continued on his way uptown, the concentration furrow deep between his brows.

For he knew very well the timber had not been dislodged by accident. When he glanced up, he distinctly saw two pairs of hands shoving the thing.

9

When Slade arrived at the Walking Beam, Ames had not yet put in an appearance and neither Marshal Otey nor the sheriff were present.

Dolores was. She greeted him shyly, the color coming and going in her softly rounded cheeks, her big eyes downcast but bright.

"You look radiant," he complimented.

"Well, why not?" she replied, with a giggle.

She plumped into a chair and gave her spangled short skirt a tug.

"It won't stay down," she complained.

"Yes."

Dolores blushed and hastily changed the subject. "I want some coffee," she said. "Have some with me."

She had just finished her coffee when Chris Ames hurried in and beckoned to her.

"Be seeing you, dear," she said to Slade. "He must have something for me to do."

A few minutes later Sheriff Young entered, with him a gangling string bean with twinkly brown eyes whom he introduced as Jim Sanborn, John Harper's range boss.

"Mighty glad to know you, Mr. Slade," Sanborn said. "But what in blazes did you do to the Old Man?"

"Why, nothing that I can recall," Slade replied.

"Well, you sure must have done something," Sanborn declared. "Soon as he got home late in the afternoon he began talking about you. Some of the boys were discussin' those cows we lost last night and somebody sorta mentioned Bill Carr's name. The Old Man hit the ceiling.

" 'I don't want to hear any more of that blabbermouthin' about Carr,' he bellered. 'If I catch anybody doin' it, I'll use a singletree on him.' I figgered he meant it. What *did* you do to him?"

The sheriff shook with laughter. "Walt just talked to him, nice and quiet," he said. "John listened."

"So it would 'pear," Lank Jim returned dryly. "But what about Carr? He's been makin' some big medicine."

"Oh, Carr caught it, too, and pulled in his horns mighty fast," chuckled the sheriff. "They both 'greed to stop blattin' about each other."

"I'm sure glad somebody was able to make 'em," sighed Lank Jim. "I never could get 'em to listen. Now maybe we can all pull together and clean out that nest of snakes that's been making all the trouble hereabouts."

"They'll be cleaned out, all right," the sheriff stated, confidently.

Sanborn regarded Slade a moment. "Yes, I think they will be," he agreed. " 'Scuse me a minute, gents, there's a feller at the bar I want to speak to."

"Jim's got sense," said the sheriff, his eyes following Sanborn's gangling form. "Harper would be better off if he listened to him more. Anything happen today?"

"Oh, nothing much, except down in the field a couple of gents tried to drop a stick of timber on my head," Slade said carelessly. He did not mention Craig Lane because he didn't wish the sheriff to be jumping to conclusions.

"The devil you say!" Young exploded. "What did you do?"

"Nothing," Slade replied. "Because I couldn't have possibly proven it was other than an accident."

"But—but what does it mean?" stuttered the bewildered peace officer.

"All I'm prepared to say at the moment is that it would appear to indicate that the bunch, a well-organized and business-like outfit, has certain of its members planted in the field, probably for the purpose of gathering information that will be helpful to them in staging their raids. No hit-and-miss methods for them; they work with the precision of a well-oiled machine. I imagine that pair thought they saw a chance to get rid of me. It didn't work."

"Nothing 'pears to work against you," the sheriff sighed. "Anybody else would have been dead a dozen times over. Spotted you as *El Halcón* with a reputation of hornin' in on good things other folks have started, eh?"

"Probably," Slade conceded.

"Think you'd know that pair if you saw them again?"

"Possibly, although I only got a glimpse of them peering over the stack of timbers," Slade replied.

"Guess a glimpse was enough for you," said the sheriff.

"They may have slipped a mite and tipped their hand a little," Slade added thoughtfully, not explaining why he believed so.

Lank Jim Sanborn returned to the table. He and Young had a couple of snorts and then wandered out to look things over. Slade ordered more coffee and relaxed comfortably, watching the dance-floor girls until Dolores should put in an appearance.

He was still alone when Bill Carr entered. With him was one of his hands who was introduced as Pete. Slade invited them to join him.

"Mr. Slade," said Carr, after he had given the waiter an order, "you know we heard quite a bit about you up in the panhandle."

"Yes?"

"Yes, and all of it good. The other night when I was in here you may have noticed one of my hands, a little fellow packing a couple of Colts about as big as he is, giving you a once-over. I'm sure you must have noticed, for you don't seem to miss anything. His name is Charley Bancroft and he used to be a tough and ornery gunslinger, gun for hire. I got hold of him and sorta straightened him out."

"After pullin' him from under a stampede and darn near getting yourself killed doing it," Pete put in.

"Never mind that," said Carr. "Yes, Charley is plumb reformed, and I figure he's a lot happier because of it. I heard him say once or twice that he knew of but one man he wouldn't want to go up against with guns or anything else— *El Halcón*."

Carr paused suggestively. Slade smiled and did not comment.

"Well," Carr continued, "the other night Charley spotted you first off, and naturally he was quite interested. Incidentally, he said he hasn't altered his opinion one bit. That's why he kept looking at you when he thought you weren't looking his way. I'm telling you this, Mr. Slade, because I didn't want you to misunderstand Charley's interest."

"I'm glad you told me," Slade said.

"And," Carr added, "I think it would please Charley an awful lot if the next time you see him you'll come over and speak to him. He sure admires you."

"I'll be glad to do so," Slade promised, and took advantage of the opening Carr had unwittingly given him.

"And I think, Mr. Carr, that it would be a good idea for you to drop in for a talk with John Harper, soon," he said.

Carr stared. "He's liable to take a shotgun to me," he demurred.

"I don't think you need worry," Slade smiled. "In fact, I feel safe in predicting he'll welcome you. You and he can compare notes relative to your recent cattle losses and perhaps hit on something of value."

Carr shook his head and looked a trifle dazed. "I don't know how the devil you do the things you do," he declared. "Okay, I'll drop in on Harper tomorrow, and I'll be glad to do so. I don't enjoy not getting along with my neighbors."

After another drink, Carr and Pete took their departure. Slade relaxed again, quite pleased with the day's work. At least he didn't have to worry about a range war blowing up around his ears. And he felt he may have moved a trifle closer to the solution of his main problem, the Cito Raiders or whoever was responsible for the depredations committed in the section.

And the motive back of the systematic looting of John Harper's stock was now not quite so obscure. He had the first inkling when he stood on the banks of Sinking Creek and gazed north.

That was now strengthened, and Slade had a shadowy notion—not too shadowy—as to who might well be the mastermind pulling the strings in the background.

The clumsy attempt on his life in the oil field had been one of those fatuous acts that will sometimes be committed by even the wisest and had given *El Halcón* his first real lead.

As to just how to follow up the lead he was at the moment uncertain. The problem was complex, and he could be wrong. On the surface, the conclusion at which he had arrived appeared a trifle ridiculous. He did not believe it was.

But believing and proving were radically different matters. Well, providing the proof was up to him. And until he did so, he must expect more overt acts and more trouble.

"Well," he told his coffee cup, "time that grinds the rocks will tell us all." He rolled another cigarette and waited for Dolores to reappear.

She did, very shortly. "Should be a quiet night," she said. "Always is the night after payday. I expect we'll close early. I hope so."

"Getting tired of your job?" he teased.

"No," she replied. "I like my work, but—"

Her roguish smile and an upward glance completed the remark.

10

The following morning, Slade rode out of Gunlock. However, he did not ride north to John Harper's ranchhouse. Instead, he headed due east until he was well away from the town. Then he turned south and continued steadily until he was close to the broken crests and rugged brush-grown slopes of the Cap Rock. He turned east again and rode very slowly. He had paid little attention to his backtrack, for on the level prairie it was impossible for anybody to follow him without being spotted while still a long way off.

While instinctively keeping a vigilant watch on his surroundings, especially those sinister slopes to the south, Slade minutely scanned the ground over which he passed. Mile after mile he covered, with Shadow pacing along at a slow walk, and found nothing. It began to look like his hunch might not be a straight one. From time to time he reined in to study the Cap Rock slopes, but always without results.

And then his tedious search was rewarded. It wasn't much. Very likely, eyes less keen would never have detected it; but it was enough for the eyes of *El Halcón*.

Just a few broken grass blades, a fresh scar on a flat outcropping of rock, a dangling twig or two;

but to Walt Slade these tiny signs told a story as clearly as the printed page. Cattle and horsemen had passed this way not long before.

A few wandering steers, rounded up and driven back to better pasture by a cowhand? No; there were no indications of grass cropping, the area covered was not wide enough, and there were indubitable signs, to the eyes of *El Halcón*, that the cattle and horses had been travelling at a fast and direct pace.

"Looks like I was right and this is it," he remarked to Shadow. "Well, horse, we'll just go and see."

Turning the big black's head he rode south toward the not very distant Cap Rock, his glance continually searching the ground and his surmise constantly being substantiated. A fair sized herd had been driven south across the rangeland.

The Cap Rock drew near, the early afternoon sun glittering on its rocks, reddening the twigs of the thick growth that clothed its upper slopes. And straight ahead were those telltale signs.

Not far from the base of the slopes, Slade drew rein, his gaze travelling upward. He uttered an exultant exclamation.

"There it is, horse," he said. "No doubt about it. There's the supposed-to-be hidden trail up which they run the cows, but where in blazes do they take them? Well, it's up to us to find out."

At the base of the slope the growth was comparatively thin, but very quickly the chaparral drew together to present a thorny wall that showed no opening.

But Slade's carping gaze, fixed on the upper slopes, noted a barely perceptible difference, something he had seen before and which he instantly identified.

Scoring the crown of the growth and curving and winding up the slope was a faint indenture, a slight hollowing in the bristly crown, not more than a couple of yards wide. And this Slade knew marked the route of a very old trail, doubtless made by marauding Indians and those who came before them.

The explanation of the peculiar manifestation was simple. In the course of the ages, myriads of moccasined feet, and feet before the advent of moccasins on the Texas scene, had beaten the ground to an iron hardness that was almost impervious to rain water. Rain ran off without penetrating the adamantine surface.

As a result, the starved growth on the trail was scanty or, for the most part, non-existent, and what was present was dwarfed. The topmost chaparral on either side gradually merged to hide the track, but the reaching branches bent slightly downward. The casual observer would never suspect that hidden beneath that slight hollowing was a negotiable track through the growth.

Walt Slade, however, had encountered such phenomena before and knew what to look for. The Texas hills, including the Cap Rock, were criss-crossed by these ancient trails, many of them lost or forgotten. He was not at all surprised to find one here. In fact, he had suspected its existence after the failure of the Walking H punchers to intercept the herd stolen a few nights before. The wideloopers blithely ran the cows south and into the Cap Rock while Harper's hands kept watch at the base of the Cito Hills.

Yes, he was convinced he had discovered the route taken by the purloined cows, but he was confronted by one very puzzling angle. Where the devil did the hellions run the cows after sliding them into the Cap Rock? To reach New Mexico and the obvious market, they would have to follow a well-travelled trail south of the Cap Rock, and it was inconceivable that they would be able to traverse the forty miles without being detected.

Well, it was up to him to learn that, too. He sent Shadow forward in line with the indentation winding up the slope.

Entering the lower growth, where the cattle and the horses had to force their way between the trunks and trailing branches, he found plenty of evidence to confirm his deductions. The herd had gone up the slope, all right, but to where? That he still had to find out.

He reached the beginning of the old trail, over which the branches interlaced; Shadow's irons rang on the hard surface. Now he rode slowly and with caution, straining his ears to catch any sound. Wouldn't be pleasant to meet the outlaw bunch coming around one of the many and abrupt turns.

But with nothing happening, gradually he worked his way up the slope. He was not far below the crest when the trail veered sharply to the west and continued parallel to the summit of the rise. He had covered fully a mile of slow going when he pulled Shadow to a halt and sat tense and alert.

To his ears had come a sound, thin with distance and muffled by the growth—the bleat of a steer. Now what the devil! He leaned forward in the saddle, straining his ears.

Again came the sound, and a moment later a third time. And Slade was convinced that its source was stationary. What that meant he was not at all sure. His caution increased as he started his mount moving again.

The sound was repeated, again and again, steadily getting louder as he drew near its source. Soon he knew he could not be far from the animal emitting the bleats and began to fear lest the beat of Shadow's irons on the hard trail be heard by listening ears.

"This won't do, feller," he told the horse. "I'm

going to have to leave you for a while. Let's see, now."

Directly ahead, the growth on the left thinned quite a bit. He turned Shadow's head and eased him along through the tangle until, only a short distance from the trail, he came to a little open space where grass grew and a trickle of water oozed from beneath a jut of rock.

"This'll do it," he murmured as he dismounted, flipped out the bit, and loosened the cinches. "You take it easy and surround a bit of grass. I'll be with you soon, I hope, and please don't go singing any songs to give the game away."

However he had little apprehension on that score; Shadow was a quiet horse. He glided back to the trail, listened a moment, then followed its course toward the sound of bleating. He covered a hundred yards or so and the growth began to thin. Leaving the trail, he eased along through the chaparral. Behind a final leafy fringe, he paused, peering and listening.

He was at the edge of a fairly large clearing. Over to one side stood an old cabin with a thatched roof, similar to many he had encountered in the wastelands, doubtless built by a hunter, trapper, or prospector or some gent with a hermit's instinct and a desire to get away from it all.

And beyond was a rough but sturdily built corral, behind the bars of which were more than three score fat beefs.

"What in blazes?" the Ranger muttered beneath his breath. "Do the hellions hole up the critters here and then run them to New Mexico at night? They could never do it, not in one night, and even at night they'd be taking a devil of a chance of being spotted. Nope, that's not the answer."

He itched to draw near the corral and examine its bovine tenants, but that silent cabin required attention first. For a long time he stood studying the ancient shack.

To all appearances it was unoccupied. No smoke rose from its stick-and-mud chimney, no shadow moved behind the dirty windowpanes. It exuded, Slade felt, that indefinable something that marks the deserted house.

But he had to be sure; a mistake would very likely prove fatal. He was somewhat reassured by the fact that there were no horses gathered beneath a nearby lean-to. That, however, was not enough; they might be grazing elsewhere. He studied the shack a little longer, listening for any sound that might indicate human occupancy, and heard none.

That, too, was not enough. If some of the outlaws were there, they could be asleep. He continued his silent watch, noting that the growth edged close to the rear of the building. There might be a back door that would provide entrance without having to cross the open ground.

With the greatest caution, he edged through

the growth until he was behind the cabin, moved forward a few steps and was disappointed to see there was no back door, only a single narrow window. And still he could hear not the slightest sound coming from inside. He made up his mind to a hazardous move.

Leaving his place of concealment, he glided to the cabin wall and flattened against it. Slowly, silently he eased along the wall, turned the corner and stole forward until he reached a wider side window. Drawing a deep breath, he risked peering through.

That quick glance showed him a fairly large room which was empty. Toward the rear was a door that doubtless led to a small inner room. He saw there were bunks built along the walls of the big room, unoccupied. There might be somebody in the back room, but he did not think so. Turning another corner he approached the closed front door and gently lifted the latch, his other hand on a gun butt.

The door swung open. Slade whisked inside and across to the inner room, guns ready for instant action, and flung open the door. A single glance showed it to be unoccupied. It boasted no furnishings other than a bunk built against the far wall and raised more than two feet from the floor. He turned to the larger room, closing the inner room door.

It had been fitted up to provide a very comfortable hangout. In addition to the bunks there was a table and several chairs, all home-made, but in good condition, very likely constructed by the former occupant of the cabin who was probably its builder. There was a stone fireplace equipped with hooks and a grid. Cooking utensils were scattered about. On shelves were staple provisions.

All this *El Halcón* noted with a quick look. He'd give the place a more careful once-over later. Now he was intensely curious about the animals in the corral, which were doubtless John Harper's cattle. Leaving the cabin and closing the door after him, he made his way to the corral, leaned against the bars and stared. Abruptly everything was crystal clear.

11

The disgusted looking occupants of the corral were John Harper's stock, all right; but they didn't bear his brand, not at the moment.

"Well, critters," *El Halcón* said, "some member of the bunch is a re-write man who is an artist with the slick iron."

Harper's Walking H had been neatly altered to a very creditable Rocking R, the burn of a reputable ranch about fifty miles to the east. Now how the wideloopers managed to run the stolen cows to the New Mexico market was painfully apparent. The brand had been so skillfully changed that only a close inspection by sharp eyes would note the deception after the burns had scabbed over a little; within less than a week the herd would be ready to roll. And nobody would pay any mind to a bunch of Rocking R cows ambling to the railroad loading pens or some other market. The Rocking R spread was so located as to be practically immune to rustling. Even if one of Harper's hands spotted the herd on the trail he would be highly unlikely to catch on. Unless he had happened to form a personal friendship with one of the critters and would recognize it on sight, a contingency Slade felt was highly remote.

Doubtless Bill Carr's C Bar C had undergone a like transformation, to an O Cross Q, or something similar.

Altogether, as impudently ingenious a scheme as Slade had ever encountered. His respect for the shrewdness of the Cito Raiders, so called, had risen.

With a final look at the altered brands, he returned to the cabin to make sure he had left no trace of his visit. He was forming a plan that he believed might work and put an end to the bunch once and for all.

Entering the cabin and closing the door, he glanced around, took a step forward and halted, every nerve tense. To his ears had come a sound. Peering out the window, he saw half a dozen horsemen riding into the clearing.

He was trapped!

Slade's brain worked at hair-trigger speed; there was only one thing to do. The odds were a bit lopsided. He whipped open the inner room door, closed it and dived under the bank, hugging the wall. If nobody entered the room, he might get by.

The outer door banged open. There was a rumble of voices. Slade could not distinguish what was said, but he thought one of the voices had a familiar ring. He snuggled against the wall and strained his ears. There were sounds

116

of moving about, a rattling of cooking utensils. Evidently somebody was throwing together a meal. Chairs scraped and creaked as men sat down. A smell of tobacco smoke drifted through a crack in the door. Apparently nobody suspected his presence or had noticed any signs of his visit to the shack.

Just the same, Slade knew he was in a very hot spot. Did somebody enter the room for some reason, it was highly unlikely that he would escape being discovered. The bunk was narrow and raised rather high from the floor. Also, it was short and he had to draw up his knees to keep his feet from sticking out, which didn't help.

For one thing he was thankful. It was nearly sunset, with darkness not far off, which might work to his advantage even did the outlaws intend to spend the night in the cabin.

The aroma of cooking food and boiling coffee seeped into the room and Slade realized he was hungry as the devil. His muscles ached from his strained position on the hard boards, but there was nothing he could do about it. He grimly endured the discomfort and schooled his soul to patience.

There was a clattering of tin plates and mugs. The rumble of voices ceased save for an occasional remark. Once again the smell of burning tobacco. A little later there was a sound

117

of pushed-back chairs and conversation began again. The voice with the familiar ring rose until Slade could make out what was said.

"All right, let's be moving," said the voice. "Wirt, you and Parker will stay here and keep an eye on the cows and things; we'll see you in the morning some time, after we pick up the rest of the boys."

Then followed a thumping of boots on the floor boards. The outer door opened and closed, after which a querulous grumbling arose in the big room; looked like Wirt and Parker were displeased at having been left behind.

Slade was also displeased at their being left behind. Had looked for a moment like he would have no trouble escaping from the shack and perhaps be able to retrieve Shadow and trail the hellions to wherever they were headed. He had a suspicion that whatever they had in mind bode no good for somebody.

At the moment, however, he had an urgent personal problem in need of attention. It was absolutely essential that he escape from the cabin before the return of the rest of the band. The odds were still unfavorable, but two against one was a devil of a sight better than six against one. So if he could just manage to get the drop on the pair in the outer room, he could capture them and perhaps induce them to do a little talking to save their own necks and provide him with badly needed information relative to the identity and activities of the bunch.

With the greatest caution to make not the slightest sound, he eased from under the bunk, stood up and flexed his muscles to relieve them of stiffness. He no longer cared if one of the occupants entered the small room for some reason or other; might well provide him with opportunity, having them separated.

From the outer room the grumbling continued, accompanied by sounds of moving about and the rattle of plates and cups as the table was cleared. After a bit there was a creaking of chairs and silence, and the drifting aroma of tobacco smoke. Slade slipped across to the door, put his eye to the crack in it.

The two men were seated at the table, smoking and looking to be in a bad temper. Facing him was a burly individual with a cast in one eye. Slade had a profile view of his companion, smaller, of slighter build, who occupied a chair at the end of the table. Slade had never seen him before, but the larger man he instantly recognized as one of the pair that had tried to drop the timber on his head in the oil field.

For a moment he studied the pair. Then he drew one gun, gripped the latch with his left hand and slowly, carefully, raised it until it was free of the slot. With a hard jerk he flung the door wide open. His voice blared at the dumbfounded pair, "Elevate! You're covered!"

For an instant they seemed paralyzed by the unexpected suddenness of the onslaught. Then the small man raised his hands, jerkily, looking dazed, his mouth hanging open.

The big man acted. Over went the table, but before he could crouch behind it, Slade shot him squarely between his glaring eyes. He fell back without a sound.

The smaller man was on his feet, blazing away at the weaving, ducking Ranger. A slug grazed Slade's cheek. A second ripped through his sleeve. He fired again and again.

His opponent gave a gasping cry. The gun dropped from his nerveless hand and he slumped to the floor beside his companion to lie motionless.

Lowering his smoking Colt, Slade gazed disgustedly at the pair. Both were stone dead and would do no talking this side of Judgment Day.

Oh, well, it could have been worse. He reloaded his gun, holstered it and dabbed at the slightly bleeding cut in his cheek. Just a scratch, nothing to bother about.

Righting the table and chairs, which fortunately had not been broken, he dragged the bodies aside and went through their pockets revealing nothing he considered significant. He speculated the floor for a moment. It was spotted with grease and other filth and he did not think the blood stains would be noticed.

On a bed of coals in the fireplace a pot of coffee simmered. Nearby was a skillet. Rummaging on the shelves he unearthed some eggs and a slab of bacon. Feeding the dying fire with a few chips from a heap that lay nearby he soon had the bacon and eggs sizzling in the skillet. A little more rummaging about uncovered some slices of bread. Drawing up a chair, he poured a cup of coffee, sat down, and enjoyed a hearty meal. After eating he rolled and lighted a cigarette and considered the situation.

As a result of his cogitations, he cleaned the utensils and placed them exactly as he had found them. On a peg driven into the wall hung a lantern. He lighted it and went outside to the lean-to where he found two horses contentedly munching oats. They regarded him mildly and went on eating. Stepping to where the trail entered the clearing, he whistled a loud and clear note. A moment or two and Shadow came pounding to him, snorting his disgust at everything in general. Slade led him to the lean-to and poured him a helpin' of oats from a nearby sack, treating the outlaws' horses to a little more. After which he returned to the cabin, sat down and smoked another cigarette while the horses consumed their surrounding.

Pinching out the butt, he dragged the two bodies outside, got the rigs on the two horses and led them to the cabin door. He roped the bodies securely to the saddles, replaced the lantern and, after a final glance about to make sure everything was in order, he blew out the bracket lamp and left the shack, closing the door behind him.

"Well, feller, here we go," he told the black as he flipped the bit into place and tightened the cinches. "Those two gents were plainly disgruntled at being left in the cabin, and showed it. So perhaps the rest of the bunch will conclude they took their spite out in riding off somewhere. Hope so. This may not work out so bad after all."

Half way down the trail he drew rein, forced his way well into the growth with the bodies and dumped them on the ground, the saddles on top, covering everything with brush.

"That should do it," he told Shadow. "Not likely anybody will unearth them there. A rather unorthodox thing for a law enforcement officer to do, but needs must when the devil drives."

Upon reaching the level ground, he led the two horses far out on the prairie. Removing the bridles he tossed them into a thicket, leaving the critters to fend comfortably for themselves until somebody picked them up. Then he headed for town, pondering the situation as it stood.

Evidently the rest of the bunch planned to return to the cabin in the morning, but there was no guarantee that they would remain there for long, and unless they did remain most of the day he could not hope to get a posse together and return to the clearing in time to apprehend them.

Also, they might become suspicious at the extended absence of their two companions and be on the *qui vive*, with the trail guarded. And he had no desire to stage a corpse and cartridge session with the advantage on their side.

He felt fairly sure the cows would not be removed from the corral for at least three or four days. Best to try and strike them then. It would be a dangerous game of hide-and-seek, but he could think of no better solution.

It was well past midnight when he reached Gunlock. Stabling his horse, he repaired to the Walking Beam where he found Dolores with a fine case of the jitters.

"You're the limit!" she scolded. "You say you're going for a little ride and vanish off the face of the earth. And, oh, darling, you're hurt! Your cheek's cut! What happened?"

"I ran into something," he replied cheerfully, that being near enough to the truth. He'd run into something, all right, or it had run into him.

He deprecated the injury, which really was very slight, but she insisted on treating it with a soothing ointment.

"You're spoiling me," he protested. "Every time I cut myself shaving you'll come running with medicants."

"If you cut yourself like that, I'll insist that you

grow a beard," she retorted. "Now I'll get you coffee and something to eat. Sheriff Young? He was in a little while ago and said he'd be back. I think he's worried about you, too."

Slade laughed. Dolores made a face at him.

She returned shortly with his dinner, then headed for the back room, where she had work to do.

While Slade was eating, Sheriff Young appeared and joined him, looking expectant. Slade told him everything, in detail. Young shook his head and swore in amazement.

"And you spotted their hang-out, and in the Cap Rock, not the Cito Hills!" he marvelled. "I wonder why nobody ever thought of that."

"Cattlemen, as a rule, are creatures of habit," Slade replied. "They follow an established routine and expect everybody else to do the same. Cows had always been run into New Mexico by way of the hills, so of course they always would be. The wideloopers tackled the chore from a different angle. I arrived with a fresh viewpoint and put it into effect. I quickly became convinced that the stolen cattle were not being run into the hills, contrary to popular opinion, and went to work on that angle. I had the luck to hit on their trail, that's all."

"Oh, sure, that's all," snorted the sheriff. "Just as easy as falling off a slick log. That is for *El Halcón*. Something nobody else in the section ever tumbled to and wouldn't have been able to follow the lead if they had.

"And that brand blotting!" he added wrathfully. "If that don't take the hide off the barn door! Those hellions have been running off cows right under my nose. But it's sure a plumb wonder you didn't get your comeuppance. If they'd spotted you while the whole bunch was in that shack! Gentlemen, hush!"

"I wasn't feeling too good about it for a while," Slade admitted, with a smile. "However, everything worked out okay, and that's all that counts. Yes, they've been rolling stolen herds right along the east-west trail to the south of the Cap Rock, under plenty of noses." The sheriff swore some more.

"All I can say is that I sure hanker to line sights with the hellions," he growled.

"Well, if things work out right, you'll get a chance to," Slade assured him. Young immediately looked interested.

"Got something figgered out, eh?" he commented.

"Yes, I believe I have," Slade said. "Here's the plan. As I said before, I feel pretty sure they won't move those cows from the corral for three or four days, not until the change of the brands is not so marked. So on the third night from tonight, have your posse ready. We'll follow the old trail to the cabin. If they are there, we'll have

125

a good chance to drop a loop on the whole bunch, including the big he-wolf of the pack. If they are not there, I figure they'll be already shoving the cows west to New Mexico. In which event we'll cross the Cap Rock by way of the old trail and light out after them. We will certainly overtake the comparatively slow moving herd before it reaches the hills. Either way we should get the jump on the horned toads."

"Sounds good," agreed the sheriff. "Don't see any reason why it won't work. Okay, I'll be ready—I'll slide my three deputies into town day after tomorrow. Them and a couple of specials oughta be enough, don't you think?"

"Plenty," Slade replied. "The element of surprise will be in our favor, even though we may be outnumbered a bit."

"Okay, then," Young repeated. "Now I'm going to bed. I stayed up late against the chance you'd amble in. Glad I did. Be seeing you."

Things were quiet. There were but a few customers at the bar, the games had mostly shut up shop and the girls were leaving the floor. Slade settled himself comfortably in his chair and waited for Dolores to put in an appearance.

12

A couple of uneventful days followed. Slade spent a good part of the time wandering around the oil field which interested him. He saw nothing of Craig Lane, the oil buyer.

In the course of his prowling about he noted a fact he considered significant. Significant in that it tended to confirm certain deductions of his own: the field, though an excellent producer, was strictly a pumper. No explosive gushers soared upward to knock derricks to pieces and splatter the surrounding territory with drops of black gold. The oil had to be pumped from the subterranean pool.

It was the evening of the second day that Craig Lane appeared while Slade was eating his dinner in the Walking Beam. He waved a greeting and smiled, pleasantly enough, before making his way to the far end of the bar where Chris Ames stood.

But it seemed to Slade that there was a derisive quality to his smile, as if Lane were hugely enjoying some little joke of his own. And it subjected the Ranger to a vague uneasiness for which he could not definitely account. What might the shrewd devil have up his sleeve, he wondered.

There was not the slightest doubt in *El Halcón*'s mind that Craig Lane was head of the Cito Raiders, the mastermind who directed their nefarious operations from his headquarters in Gunlock.

He had come to regard the announced oil buyer as the only logical suspect he had encountered even before Lane made the fatal slip of signalling the derrick worker to drop the timber on his head that confirmed his deductions.

Also, he was confident that he had read aright Lane's secret and knew what was the huge stake for which he was playing, for which by robbery and murder he was amassing the money necessary to swing the deal.

Lane did not stay long. After he departed, Chris Ames came over to join Slade.

"Lane is feeling sorta chipper," he announced. "Seems he's just about closed deals with a couple of drillers for their output. The first real break he's got, I reckon."

Slade nodded and did not comment. He hoped Ames was right in his surmise as to why Craig Lane was in such a jovial frame of mind, but he was frankly dubious.

It was well past dark the evening of the third day when the posse, Slade and the sheriff leading, rode out of Gunlock. They covered the open prairie at a fast pace but slowed down decidedly as they climbed the trail that slithered into the stony heart of the Cap Rock. For Slade was taking no chances on a slip that might easily prove disastrous.

However, nothing happened. Some little distance from the clearing, Slade drew rein, the others jostling to a halt behind him.

"Stay here and keep the horses quiet," he told them. "I'm going to slide ahead on foot for a look."

With the greatest caution, pausing often to peer and listen, he worked his way to the clearing. At its edge he halted, staring incredulously.

The corral was empty, the gate bars down. Where the cabin had stood was but a heap of ashes, the remains of the chimney and a few charred and blackened beams.

After studying the clearing for some moments, by the light of the late moon, he approached the ruins of the cabin. An examination showed him it had been fired some days before. Thoroughly disgusted, he returned to his companions.

"I was outsmarted, that is all," he concluded after telling them what he discovered. "The devil is even shrewder than I gave him credit for being. Somehow he caught on to or suspected what happened in the cabin the other night. So he set fire to the shack, knowing he'd never use it again, and hightailed with the cows, taking a chance on the fresh brands. Not much of a chance to take, incidentally. Yes, he's got plenty of wrinkles on his horns and put it over on me very neatly."

"Think we ought to make for the east-west trail on the chance we might catch up with the hellions?" asked Young.

"Would be just a waste of time and a long and hard ride for nothing," Slade answered. "Several days since he set the torch to the cabin. Those cows were in New Mexico long ago and are well on the way to becoming beefsteaks. I'd hoped to return the herd to John Harper, but after all the loss may not mean too much."

This somewhat cryptic remark he did not amplify.

"Don't go blaming yourself for what happened," Sheriff Young comforted as they headed for home. "Nobody can figure everything in advance, and we all agree you handled the business as it looked like it should be handled."

"I suppose so," Slade conceded wearily. "But that sidewinder is still running loose and all set to make more trouble. I wager we'll hear from him soon and won't like what we hear."

"Uh-huh, maybe so, but I figure the next time he won't slide out of the loop," the sheriff predicted confidently.

It was not long to daybreak when they reached Gunlock, but Slade found Dolores waiting for him.

He was glad she was, for he felt the need of a little consolation. He didn't lack for it.

Slade took it easy the rest of the day and the night that followed, but the next morning found him riding north to visit John Harper, as he promised he would. After fording Sinking Creek, he turned and gazed back toward the oil field.

"Horse, I'm right," he told Shadow. "I'll bet your left hind leg I am."

"Don't try to take it off," Shadow's answering snort seemed to warn. "You've got a nice set of front teeth; keep 'em that way."

Slade chuckled and rode on.

It was a beautiful morning and he took his time, admiring the excellence of the rangeland he crossed. John Harper had a holding to be proud of.

Old John was sitting on the veranda soaking up sunshine when Slade pulled rein in front of his big house. He let out a bellow of welcome and bawled for a wrangler who came running, was introduced to Shadow and led the big black off to a stall and oats.

"Come on in, come on in," said Harper. "I'll have coffee and a snack for us in a jiffy.

"Manuel!" he shouted, as he led the way into the comfortably furnished living room.

An old Mexican appeared in the doorway. He stared at *El Halcón*, bowed low and smiled. He smiled again, happily, as Slade voiced a Spanish greeting. Old John glanced from one to the other.

"Rattle your hocks, Manuel, and throw something together for us," he ordered. The cook bowed again and hurried back to his kitchen.

"Been with me for nigh onto forty years," Harper said, jerking his thumb toward Manuel's departing form. "A plumb smart *hombre*. I set a heap of store by him and anything he says.

"Bill Carr was over to see me the other day," he continued. "Said you sent him. Glad you did. Funny how things work out, ain't it? Carr's folks sprung up in Henderson County, Trinity River country, where my folks first settled—I get back there for a visit every now and then. We found we knew quite a few fellers in common. He's all right."

"Most folks are, once you get to know them," Slade smiled.

"If you say it, guess it's so," Harper conceded.

"You have a fine holding, Mr. Harper," Slade commented, glancing around.

"Yes, it is," Harper agreed, "but I'm scairt I'll have to let go of some of it," he added regretfully. "I wouldn't mind too much if somebody would make me an offer for the south pasture. I'd let go of that without feeling too bad about it."

Slade leaned forward in his chair, his steady eyes hard on Harper's face.

"Don't," he said.

"Huh? How's that?" Harper replied.

"Don't," Slade repeated impressively. "Don't

sell that land, no matter how attractive an offer somebody may make. Hang onto it."

"But—but," stuttered the bewildered rancher, "it ain't much good, now—"

"Mr. Harper," Slade interrupted, "the contention that oil fumes kill cattle and oil poisons them is nothing but rank superstition. Oil fumes do *not* kill cattle, and a little oil slick on the water they drink does them no harm; they don't even notice it. And I'll tell you something. That stretch of land is very likely far and away the most valuable of your property."

Old John sighed, and repeated his former remark, "If you say it, I guess it's so. Okay, I won't sell. But," he added gloomily, "if things don't pick up, I may lose the whole kit and kaboodle."

"You will not," Slade stated positively. "And, Mr. Harper, I'd like to ask you a favor."

"Anything you want," Harper replied instantly. "What is it?"

Slade spoke slowly, spacing his words. "If somebody makes you an offer for that south pasture, please let me know at once, and who makes the offer. Say you haven't made up your mind about selling and will think it over, and get word to me immediately."

"Okay," Harper answered. "I sure don't know what you're driving at, but I'll do just as you say."

Suddenly his lips twitched in a quizzical grin. "Slade," he chuckled, "do you always make folks do just what you tell them to?"

"I fear not everybody," Slade replied smilingly.

"I figure them that don't need their heads examined," old John declared with conviction.

"Come in, Jim," he called as Lank Jim Sanborn's gangling form loomed in the outer door. "You remember Slade, of course?"

"Guess I do," answered Lank Jim. "He ain't easy to forget. How are you, Slade? Sorry to see you in such bad company."

"He wasn't a minute ago, but I guess he is now," Harper retorted.

Having mutually affronted each other, they filled their pipes and lit up. Slade rolled another cigarette.

A little later, Manuel called them to the "snack," which proved to be quite a snack.

"Guess the old jigger thinks it's Christmas," chuckled Harper, glancing at the loaded table.

"*Patron*," said Manuel from the kitchen door, bowing again to Slade, "*Patron*, this also is a day!"

"I've a notion you're right," Harper agreed soberly.

13

Walt Slade rode back to Gunlock, through the blue and gold shadows of evening, feeling that his visit to the Walking H had been well worth while. He believed he had guaranteed that John Harper would not be cheated out of a fortune, no matter what happened. Which was something.

However, where his main objective was concerned, he experienced an irritating sense of frustration. Craig Lane and his Cito Raiders were still at large, still a source of potential trouble. Until they were done away with, one way or another, the mission on which he had been dispatched was not consummated.

It was all very well for Sheriff Young to maintain he was thinning out the hellions, had them on the run and had curtailed if not altogether ended their widelooping activities. Perhaps so, but that was not enough. He still had a chore to do, and at the moment had not the slightest notion how to do it.

Oh, well! Things would probably work out; they always did. He rode on in a peaceful frame of mind.

But as the lights of Gunlock came into view, he grew thoughtful. Once again he reined in on the bank of Sinking Creek and sat gazing at the rippling water glinting in the starshine. He shifted his eyes to the dark loom of the Cito Hills, let them travel over the rangeland, glanced toward the oil field, the elevation of which was considerably lower than the prairie to the north.

In his mind a plan was taking form, a plan that might well provide a solution to the problem that vexed him.

"Shadow," he said as he put the black to the stream, "I believe it might work. Can't see that there's anything to lose. I'll think out the angles a little more and perhaps put it into effect, after a bit. Let's go, horse, time to put on the nosebag."

When he reached the Walking Beam, Slade got Chris Ames alone.

"Chris," he said, "I believe you once told me that you are acquainted with some of the well owners down at the field. Right?"

"Yep, I know quite a few of 'em," Ames replied.

"And," Slade continued, "do you happen to know one who is competent, absolutely trustworthy, can keep a tight latigo on his jaw and who doesn't mind doing a little gambling?"

"Sure," answered Ames, "There's Dave Benedict, who brought in the first well here. He drilled when other oil men were dubious about the section and figured it would never amount to much. He's good at taking chances, keeps his mouth shut and knows all the angles of the drilling business. As I said, nobody thought much of the section where oil was concerned, but Dave brought in a shallow well and the rush was on."

"A shallow well," Slade repeated, "and a pumper."

"That's right," said Ames. "What you getting at, Walt?"

"Chris," the Ranger replied, "I'd like to have a talk with Benedict. Think you can arrange it?"

"Why, sure," the saloonman instantly responded. He glanced at the clock.

"Tell you what," he said. "Suppose we walk down to the field now. I'm pretty sure Dave will be in his office, checking up on the day. He most always is at this time of the evening. Okay?"

"That will be fine," Slade replied. "Let's go."

They found Benedict in his office as Ames predicted. He proved to be a stocky, middle-aged man with twinkling brown eyes and a humorous mouth. Slade liked his looks at once.

Ames performed the introductions and Benedict glanced questioningly at Slade as he waved them to chairs.

"Mr. Benedict," the Ranger said, "what I'm going to tell you may sound a little startling, and you may be, not unnaturally, somewhat incredulous at first. So I'd like to ask you a question before I begin."

"Shoot," said Benedict.

137

"You doubtless have heard of former governor Jim Hogg, Bet-a-Million Gates, J. S. Cullinan, and James Swain, who control such vast interests in the Beaumont field and the Port Arthur refineries?"

"Sure," answered Benedict, "What oil man hasn't? I met Hogg once, liked him. Why?"

"Because," Slade explained, "after hearing what I have to say, you may feel the need of some references relative to myself. You might send any one or all of those gentlemen a wire mentioning my name."

For several moments, Benedict regarded *El Halcón* with his twinkly, shrewd brown eyes. Abruptly he grinned.

"Isn't necessary," he said. "Chris vouches for you, and I'm very well satisfied with what I see. Go ahead and let's hear what you have to say."

Slade began talking. Benedict did look incredulous, at first. Gradually, however, his expression changed to one of intense interest. He leaned forward in his chair, so as not to miss a word.

"You're sure?" he asked when the Ranger paused.

"Here is a little more corroborative evidence," Slade answered.

As he laid it before the oil man, Benedict's expression changed again, to one of animation; his eyes snapped with excitement.

"You're a geologist, aren't you, Mr. Slade?" he said.

"I know something of the principles of geology," Slade admitted.

"Something!" Benedict chuckled. "I'd say you're the feller who wrote the book. I never heard of anything like what you just told me."

"It is a somewhat peculiar phenomenon," Slade replied. "However, it is not altogether unique. I once saw a condition somewhat similar."

Benedict hammered the table with a big fist. "By gosh, I figure you're plumb right on all counts," he declared. "I'll string along with you, Mr. Slade, whenever you give the word. And much obliged for letting me in on the ground floor. This is going to mean plenty; I'll bet my bottom dollar on it."

"You will be gambling a few," Slade smiled.

"It ain't gambling when you're playing a sure thing," Benedict said sturdily.

"I wonder why nobody else ever thought of it before?" he added reflectively. "Of course, though, the boys here are all just practical oil men who can usually read surface indications aright but who haven't the geological knowledge necessary to understand what you did."

"Somebody else has thought of it," Slade replied grimly. "That's why I am anxious to get things moving as soon as is practical."

"I'll string along with you," Benedict repeated. "You'll take care of all the details?"

"Yes," Slade promised, "and I don't anticipate

any real difficulty; only it won't do to hold off too long. Something unforeseen might occur."

"Whenever you give the word," said Benedict. "I'm rarin' to go."

Chris Ames was silent for quite a while after they left the office. Suddenly he asked, "Walt, what will you get out of this?"

"The satisfaction of lending some worthy people a helping hand," Slade replied smilingly. Ames shook his head resignedly.

"You're a hard jigger to understand," he said. "You don't seem to care a hoot for the things most men would give half their lives for."

"Too many people give not only half but all their lives for things that at the last mean nothing," *El Halcón* answered. "Getting too much breeds a hankering to get still more. The price paid is loss of contentment, of real happiness."

"I think I can understand that," Ames said slowly. "Real happiness consists of being content with what you have and not wishing too hard for more."

"Exactly," Slade agreed.

"You're a young feller, but sometimes you talk like a mighty old one," Ames commented.

"Contact with the seamy side of life is apt to age one," Slade said.

"Didn't mean it just that way," Ames replied. "I don't think *aged* applies. A man can be young in the right ways, as you are, but old in experience and understanding. Lots of young fellers get plenty of experience in a hurry, but understanding is something else. Too many never get it. Because of which they miss one hell of a lot."

His eyes brightened. "Well, here we are at the old Walking Beam!" he exclaimed. Slade smiled.

"I think, Chris," he said, "that you are one who has received the divine gift. You are perfectly satisfied with your modest holding here and don't hanker to be an oil tycoon."

"Guess you have something there," Ames chuckled. "I do like the Walking Beam and wouldn't want to leave it. Come on in before Dolores gives me hell for keeping you away."

She didn't, and took it out on Slade.

"Why did you have to go wandering off without your dinner?" she scolded. "You must be starved after riding all day."

"I had quite a snack up at John Harper's place," he protested. "That sorta stuck to my ribs."

"When?" she asked.

"Oh, a little before noon."

"And look what time it is now," she retorted. "All right, I'm going to the kitchen to see you get something before you topple over from hunger."

"Okay, I expect I'll need all my strength," he conceded.

Dolores dimpled and smiled and evidently

141

decided that the remark, while of interest, did not require an answer. She trotted off to the kitchen.

"I waited to eat with you," she called over her shoulder.

Slade finished his dinner and was smoking a cigarette when the inevitable happened, as he knew it would sooner or later.

The orchestra leader crossed the room, bowing and smiling and bearing a guitar. He paused at the table, with a very low bow.

"*Cápitan* will sing for us?" he asked.

"Yes, dear, please do," Dolores urged. "Pablo says you have a wonderful voice."

"Okay, if the crowd doesn't object," Slade replied, accepting the guitar.

"The crowd will not object," Pablo stated flatly, fingering the haft of the long knife stuck in his belt, which was part of his *charro* costume, an ominous glitter in his snapping black eyes. Slade chuckled and followed him to the little raised platform that accommodated the orchestra. Pablo held up his hand. The babble of conversation ceased.

"*Cápitan* will sing," he announced. With another low bow to Slade he retired; the crowd stood expectant. Slade ran his slender fingers over the strings of the guitar with crisp power, played a soft prelude and then threw back his black head and sang. Sang in a voice, as the poetic Pablo said, "like golden wine gushing into

142

a crystal goblet, like the unheard greeting of the Texas bluebells to the morning sun."

First, in deference to the cowhands present, a gay old ballad of the rangeland, the beauty of its sunshine, the terror of its storms, a song the riders loved.

And as the great metallic baritone-bass pealed and thundered, all activities ceased and the listeners stood entranced. With a crash of chords the music ceased and was followed by a thunderclap of applause and shouts for another.

There were many oil field men among the crowd, so he sang a song of the workers that typified those restless rovers who dared earth's wrath to filch her treasure from the shadowy depths of her stony heart, the guitar beating out an accompaniment filled with the churn of the bits through the stubborn rock, the clang of the walking beams, and the growl of the hoisting engines.

Turning, he smiled at the dance-floor girls and concluded with a composition of his own, lovely, haunting, wistful and sad, but ending on a note of up-springing joy. And the silence that sustained for a moment was a greater tribute to the singer than the applause that followed.

"Ai! He sings as sang the Heavenly Host," murmured an old Mexican. "But when he sings, let some evil one beware. For such the voice of *El Halcón* is the voice of doom."

14

There were tears on Dolores's lashes when Slade returned to the table, but she said nothing, only placed her little hand in his.

Slade would have been pleased had he overheard the old Mexican's remark, but a moment later he might have wondered did his voice have the power to conjure up the devil.

Dolores had just joined the girls on the dancefloor when Craig Lane entered. Glancing about, he spotted *El Halcón*, waved a greeting, smiled pleasantly, and sauntered to the far end of the bar.

Slade was suddenly enveloped in a flame of wrath. He did not relish being poked fun at, and he felt that was just what Lane was doing. Then his sense of humor came to the rescue and he grinned.

He who laughs last laughs best, was an old and trite saying but it might apply. He arrived at a swift decision. Waving to Dolores, he left the saloon.

However, he didn't go far, just up the street a few paces, across to the other side, where he took up his post in the dark and narrow doorway of a closed shop, where even anyone passing close by would not be likely to observe him.

Perhaps ten minutes passed before Lane put

in an appearance. He walked swiftly down the street, apparently headed for the southwest section of town.

Slade drifted along after him. There were not many people on the street and he had no difficulty keeping his quarry in view. With his own unusual eyesight he was sure he could trail his man and not be spotted by him, even did he glance back, which Lane never did. Slade had a feeling he was going to meet with some of his bunch, perhaps even to lead them on a raid. Could he trail him to his destination, he might learn something of value, possibly get a chance to drop a loop on the slippery devil. Worth trying, anyhow.

Lane turned a corner. Slade quickened his pace and followed. He sighted Lane who continued down the street that slanted toward the field. Abruptly he turned another corner into a poorly lighted street of dark warehouses and closed shops. Slade turned the corner and halted. Lane was nowhere in sight.

Now what the devil! Lane could not possibly have reached the next corner, which was quite a distance away. Where in blazes had he vanished to.

Then, his gaze roving in every direction, Slade saw that only a few paces ahead was the shadowy mouth of a narrow alley; Lane must have turned into it.

He glided forward, watchful and alert, hugging

the building wall till he reached the alley. Halting at its edge, he cautiously peered into the opening, went backward in a catlike leap as a gun blazed almost in his face. In the split second of time vouch-safed him, his keen eyes had caught the gleam of shifted metal.

Slade hesitated a moment, then, a gun trained on the alley mouth, he edged forward again, every sense at hair-trigger alert, straining the ears that could catch the sound even of hurried breathing. Once more he reached the edge of the alley, hesitated another instant, then risked a quick glance.

There was nobody in sight; but now he saw that there were narrow open spaces between the buildings which backed on the alley. Into one of them Lane had evidently slipped. Anyhow he was nowhere to be seen.

For a moment or two, Slade debated entering the alley and searching the openings between the buildings, but sober judgment told him to do nothing of the sort. Were Lane holed up in one of the cracks, waiting for him to appear, it would be just a convenient way to commit suicide.

Not that he really believed Lane was holed up anywhere in the vicinity. He felt fairly confident that he had hightailed when he realized his shot had missed, knowing Slade would reapproach the alley slowly, affording him ample time in which to escape.

Walt Slade headed back to the Walking Beam in a very bad temper. Once again he had been neatly outsmarted. Despite all his care, Lane had spotted him. Or perhaps he figured just what he, Slade, had in mind when he left the saloon. Despite the failure of his attempt at murder, Lane still had the last laugh.

El Halcón would not have been at all surprised if when he reached the Walking Beam he found Craig Lane comfortably ensconced at the bar, his derisive smile in perfect working order.

He didn't. Apparently the psuedo oil buyer had decided to let well enough alone. Slade found a vacant table, sat down and ordered a drink; he felt he needed one.

It helped. Dolores leaving the floor to sit with him helped more. Very quickly his normally optimistic viewpoint regained the ascendancy. Things hadn't worked out too bad, and in fact he was forced to admit that he rather enjoyed this deadly game of tag he and Craig Lane were playing. Were it not for the danger to others involved, he would fully enjoy it. But Lane had proven himself a ruthless killer who would not hesitate to commit murder did he feel it was to his advantage to do so.

He wondered just how much the canny devil had guessed. That he was convinced that *El Halcón* was in the section to horn in on his activities it was logical to believe and as such he was a menace that must be eliminated as quickly as possible.

But was that all? Did Lane realize that he, Slade, had divined his main objective, which was neither widelooping nor robbery? Those were but a means to an end, providing the money necessary to consummate his scheme.

And if so, there was a counter-move Lane could make, did it occur to him. And Slade uneasily believed that Craig Lane missed no bets and that it would occur to him, if it hadn't already.

In which case, John Harper would be in deadly danger. For in sheer desperation, Lane might well put the countermove into effect despite the risk involved.

If John Harper should suddenly die, there was no doubt but the bank would foreclose his mortgage and put his land up for sale with, so far as anybody could see, no takers in an already land-poor section. The bank would gladly accept anything like a reasonable offer and on liberal terms.

However, Slade did not believe that Lane would put the move into effect except as a last resort, for it might lay him open to suspicion he wouldn't relish.

All of which caused Slade to hesitate to start the wheels of his own plan turning; premature action on his part might well prove fatal. He'd hold off a little longer in the hope of a chance to drop his loop on Lane.

He wondered just what was Craig Lane's background. His dress hinted at the gambling profession. Perhaps he had been a dealer on the Mississippi or Sabine river boats, or in Beaumont, where he had familiarized himself with the oil business.

However, either Lane or somebody associated with him—Slade believed Lane himself—was something quite different from a professional gambler. He undoubtedly possessed a certain knowledge of geology. Either that or he had contacted somewhere a condition similar to the one here and had recognized the fact.

Well, that mattered little. The paramount fact was that Craig Lane was a vicious outlaw and it was his business as a Texas Ranger to see to it that he was put out of business. Other matters were purely incidental to that, his main objective.

He wondered where Lane and his bunch would strike next, for he was confident that they would strike again, and soon.

He was right.

Dolores was in a gay mood, vivacious, animated. She glanced toward the orchestra.

"Pablo and the boys are in fine form tonight, even though it is late," she said. "The music is wonderful. Come on, dance with me."

Slade was agreeable and they had several

fast numbers together. Her cheeks were rosily flushed, her eyes sparkling when they returned to the table. She glanced at the clock.

"Anticipation often surpasses realization," he teased. Dolores tossed her curls.

"But not always," she retorted. "I *know!*"

15

Shortly before noon the next day, Slade contacted Sheriff Young, who had also dropped in at the Walking Beam for breakfast.

"Was playing cards with some jiggers over at the hotel and was up all hours," he explained his tardiness. "Well, what's new?"

Slade told him, relating the happenings of the night before in detail.

At mention of Craig Lane, the sheriff at first was shocked and somewhat incredulous. But when Slade laid his proof before him, his doubt changed to outraged wrath.

"The murderin' son of a hyderphobia skunk!" he stormed, but under his breath. "So he figured to rob old John, eh?"

"He did and is still figuring to," Slade replied. "And he has been robbing him blind, cattle-wise; it is doubtful, with things as they are, that Harper could right now meet his note at the bank when it falls due. Certainly not if he suffers more losses. That is if he should have to depend on his cattle that are fit for market.

"That, of course, is why Lane has been concentrating on Harper's ranch. The New Mexico clandestine markets are much more accessible from the spreads farther north, but they have not suffered losses to amount to anything. That was something that had me puzzled from the beginning. Appeared there was a set purpose in the steady drain of Harper's resources. Then when I spotted the peculiar geological conditions here, I saw the motive."

"Bill Carr lost some cows, too," Young remarked. "For the same reason?"

Slade shook his head.

"Carr's losses were also negligible," he pointed out. "That was for the purpose of furthering the feud between the Walking H and the C Bar C. Lane hoped it could possibly get the two outfits into a corpse and cartridge session that might work to his advantage."

"How'd you catch on to the hellion in the first place?" Young asked.

"I became interested in Lane when I heard he claimed to represent Beaumont and Port Arthur interests," Slade explained. "I am thoroughly conversant with conditions in both Beaumont and Port Arthur and I very well knew that Gunlock oil offers no inducements to the interests there. They have their hands full and more than full with the vast Beaumont output and are certainly not concerned with more oil that would have to be shipped clear across Texas.

"Right then, of course, I had no idea that Lane was mixed up with the Cito Raiders or any other outlaw bunch; I just felt there was something off-color about him because he claimed to be something that I knew he definitely was not. And it has been my experience that gentlemen of that brand will bear watching. Only after I had observed and studied geological conditions here did I begin to really wonder about him. Then he made the slip his sort always seems to make sooner or later. I told you about the attempt to kill me down in the field with that derrick timber, but I didn't mention that Lane was with me at the time and that I was positive he signalled his two hellions on the platform to drop the stick. A clumsy thing for him to do, but I repeat, his sort sooner or later always makes just such a slip."

The sheriff did a little fancy swearing, in low tones.

"After that," Slade resumed, "I recalled some other incidents that all of a sudden were significant. Lane was present just before the try was made to do for me in the room over the Walking Beam. He was also in evidence before and after those two sidewinders staged the phony gunfight near the Buzzard Bait saloon; things were beginning to shape up. When I lay hidden under the bunk in the Cap Rock cabin, I was sure I recognized one of the voices as Lane's voice. Unfortunately it was impossible for me to get a look at the hellion."

"Of course last night he cinched the case

against him by trying to kill me while I was trailing him."

The sheriff swore again. "And what are we going to do about it?" he demanded.

"There is nothing we can do about it at present," Slade answered. "There is not an iota of proof against Lane that would stand up in court. So far he's been able to keep in the clear. We'll just have to wait till we get him dead to rights, somehow."

"And you really figure there is oil under Harper's land?"

"There is," Slade stated flatly. "The main reservoir is under his land, at a much greater depth than the shallow Gunlock pumping field. The Gunlock pool is nothing but seepage from the main reservoir over the course of ages. The constant jarring of the Gunlock drilling operations has caused additional very slight seepage which is responsible for the faint oil slick on the waters of Sinking Creek. There is a fortune under Harper's land, and I wouldn't be surprised if the reservoir extends under Bill Carr's land, too."

"Wonder why nobody else ever guessed it, aside from that blankety-blank Lane?"

"For two reasons, I'd say," Slade explained. "First, lack of the necessary geological knowledge to read aright the rather peculiar manifestations of a particular formation. Secondly, the oil men here are concentrating on the Gunlock field and giving no thought to other possible deposits. As I told Dave Benedict, I once before contacted a somewhat similar condition, and managed to thwart an off-color outfit that was trying to gain control by means that were dubious, to put it mildly."

"So it looks like old John may be settin' purty after all," Young commented. "Why don't you start Benedict drilling right away?"

Slade countered with a question of his own. "What would happen to the Walking H spread if Harper was to die suddenly?"

"Why—why I reckon the bank would foreclose and put the land up for sale at the face value of the mortgage. And so far as I know Harper would leave no heirs; I understand all his folks are dead."

"Exactly," Slade said. Young stared as he understood.

"You mean the hellion might try to do John in?"

"I am very much of that opinion," Slade replied grimly.

"But—but," sputtered the sheriff, "if Benedict was drilling wouldn't somebody at the field overbid for the holding?"

"Highly unlikely," Slade answered. "As I said, Benedict is going to have to drill deep to pass through the rock and tap the pool. Long before he reaches it, most folks at the field and elsewhere are going to say he's plumb loco. Yes, I firmly believe that, if he's still running loose, Lane would very likely try to kill Harper, as a last resort, and he's shrewd enough to possibly get by with it. And I can't afford to take chances on Harper's life."

Young threw out his hands despairingly and said some things anent Craig Lane that wouldn't sound nice in mixed company.

"So it's up to me to tangle the hellion's twine for him, and right now I haven't the least notion how to do it," Slade concluded.

"You'll do it, I got no doubt about that," Young growled. "Well, I'm going out for a breath of fresh air—I need it. I've got me a room over at the hotel and I'm staying right here till things clear up, in case you might want me in a hurry. I'll be seeing you later."

After the sheriff departed, Slade sauntered over for a few words with Chris Ames.

"Craig Lane been in?" he asked casually.

"Why, yes, he was here for his breakfast, as usual," Ames replied. "Said he'd be out of town for a few days—going over east to attend to some business matter, I gathered. He's always on the go."

Slade nodded, and after a little more conversation left the saloon.

Outside he stood for some moments gazing

at the loom of the Cito Hills, his black brows drawing together. Abruptly he turned and hurried to the livery stable where he kept Shadow.

"Feller," he told the big black as he cinched the saddle into place, "I'm going to play another hunch. Maybe a loco one, as I reckon you're thinking right now, but I'm going to play it. Nice day for a ride, anyhow."

For quite a while, Slade rode north. Finally, with a searching glance around the deserted prairie, he turned west and continued until he reached the Cito Hills. Then he turned and rode slowly, parallel to their base. He entered canyons and ravines, scanning their floors with the greatest care, and discovering nothing. It was not until he was well to the north and sunset wasn't far off that he struck what he considered to be paydirt. In a narrow canyon he found indubitable evidence that horses and cows had passed that way.

Not recently, to be sure, but they had gone through. Which was not surprising. It was admitted that in the past wide-looped cattle had been driven into the hills and on to the New Mexico markets.

He followed the tracks for quite some distance and became convinced that the canyon wound on right through the hills to the open ground beyond. He turned and rode back the way he had come.

"Shadow," he said, "I believe this is it. Of

course Lane can no longer drive blotted-brand cows along the east-west trail south of the Cap Rock. Because of which, everybody, including the sheriff feels sure a crimp has been put in the rustling and vigilance is relaxed. Which Craig Lane will know as well as anybody else. So now comes the hunch part, and I'm more confident than ever that the hunch is a straight one. Now all we have to do is find a place to hole up and watch, and hope luck will look our way."

Well out on the prairie he found a spot he considered suitable, a straggle of thicket. Nearby ran a little stream, one of many that wound across the rangeland to join with Sinking Creek. So he wouldn't have to make a dry camp. At the edge of the thicket he drew rein and sat gazing back at the hills.

Those hills held a never ending fascination for Walt Slade, typifying as they did the waste-lands he loved. Right now, with the night fast approaching, they were garnished in no earthly colors—rose-lighted on the billowy slopes and pearl in the clefts of canyons and ravines. One lordly spire was shrouded in indigo against a flame of orange. And gradually the orange faded, by the subtlest of color changes, to azure, in which swam a silver evening star. Slade drew a deep breath and entered the thicket.

Flipping out the bit and loosening the cinches, he dumped a helping of oats from his saddle pouches for Shadow to munch. Confident that the trickle of smoke would not be noted against the deepening shades of evening, he kindled a small fire of dry wood, over which bacon and eggs sizzled in a small skillet and coffee bubbled in a little flat bucket. With some slices of bread, this provided a simple but nourishing repast.

After which he stretched out beside the embers of the fire with a cigarette and gave himself over to thought.

His hunch, as he termed it, was in truth the result of logical deduction. Craig Lane's main objective was the financial crippling of John Harper, so it was reasonable to believe that he would pass up no opportunity to achieve that end. With everybody, except *El Halcón*, basking in the pleasant warmth of a false security, he could strike a quick blow with little risk to himself. Or so Slade hoped and believed he would think.

"But the horned toad slipped again, a little," he told Shadow. "With no real reason for doing so, he announced to Chris Ames that he planned to be out of town for a few days, on business over east, as he phrased it. He didn't need to do that; if he just hadn't showed up at his usual haunts tonight, I would have given it no thought. Plenty of places in Gunlock where he could have reasonably been expected to be; the Walking Beam is not the only saloon or restaurant in town. Informing Ames that he intended to be absent for a few days at once set me to thinking. As a result, you and I are squatting in a thicket, hoping I've guessed right. I believe I have and that we will hear from *amigo* Lane before daylight. So take it easy, horse, all we can do is wait—and hope."

The embers of the fire died to a gray ash. Slade got up and walked to the edge of the thicket, where he stood wondering at the vastness of the silence. Very lovely, in the soft star sheen—the wide expanse of hill, plain, and forest on the slopes. More like some twilight vision of a dream, some faint reflection of a fair world of peace, devoid of greed, covetousness, and ruthless disregard for the rights of others, than the familiar face of earth made silvery soft with night. He rolled a cigarette and gazed on the beautiful scene that soon might be desecrated by passion and violence. He walked back to his comfortable couch on the grass and stretched out for a little more rest.

16

The slow hours dragged past. Finally the late moon arose and very quickly the whole vista was almost as bright as day. Slade returned to the edge of the thicket and walked out a little ways to where he had a clear view in all directions.

He glanced toward the black canyon mouth, which was nearly a half mile distant, not too far and not too near for the strategy he planned. The odds would very likely be five or six to one against him, but mounted on Shadow, with his high-power Winchester and his remarkable eyesight, he was fairly sanguine as to the outcome. That is, barring one of the unforeseen accidents always an ever-present hazard in this deadly game.

Another half hour passed, slowly, with nothing happening; Slade began to wonder a little. Had he guessed wrong? Looked sort of that way. He grew acutely uneasy as fifteen minutes more dragged past.

Then far to the east a shadow developed, a moving shadow, formless at first, that rolled steadily forward. Slade slipped back into the thicket, tightened the rig and mounted. At the edge of the brush he reined in where he and the horse would merge with it. Now the shadow had developed to a herd of cattle that moved toward him at a good pace.

It was a big herd, nearly two hundred head, he estimated. Evidently the wideloopers, having little fear of interruption, had combed a number of waterholes where the cows would bunch at this time of night. Slade judged it would pass his place of concealment about four hundred yards to the south, good shooting distance in the clear moonlight. A few more minutes and he rode forward to where he would have a clear view and could himself be seen from the vicinity of the herd, indistinctly. He was a law enforcement officer and must give the hellions a chance to surrender, although there was little likelihood of them doing so.

He could hardly shout to them that they were covered, to elevate, so as the herd, paralleling the thicket, drew near, he raised his rifle and sent a slug whining in front of the five men he could now see were shoving the cows along.

Heads jerked in his direction. Another instant and there was a flicker of flame; slugs whined past. But the back of a moving horse dodging demoralized cattle is not a good shooting stance and none came close. Slade pulled trigger again and knew his bullet came within inches of the foremost rider. That was the last warning. His face set in bleak lines, his eyes the cold gray of a glacier lake under a cloudy winter sky, he steadied the rifle.

Two of the horsemen disengaged from the herd, whirled their mounts and came charging toward him. Which was very much of a mistake on their part. The Winchester's front sight came down in the notch, down and down. Slade squeezed the trigger.

The heavy rifle bucked against his shoulder, spouted flame. The foremost rider spun from the saddle to lie motionless. The other fired his rifle; the slug fanned Slade's face.

Once again that glittering front sight came steadily down, and down, and down until it was but a thin gleam of reflected moonlight in the notch. And again the black muzzle spouted flame.

The charging rider raised from the hull and slowly toppled sideways. One foot caught in the stirrup and the frantic horse went racing across the prairie, the body of the rider jumping and thudding against the ground. If the bullet didn't do for him, the horse would take care of what remained.

Now the herd was almost opposite the thicket. The distance had shrunk and abruptly Slade felt the hot burn of lead grazing his left arm. He swung the rifle around, took quick aim and fired, and again.

One of the remaining mounted men lunged far back in the saddle, almost onto the crupper, but

165

managed to right himself, grip the saddle horn and stay in the hull.

That was a bellyful for the wideloopers. With their wounded companion lurching and swaying but keeping pace, the two so far untouched sent their horses around the milling herd and skalley-hooting for the canyon.

The distance was too great to distinguish features, but Slade felt sure that one, tall, broad-shouldered, sitting his mount with easy grace, was Craig Lane. The Winchester jutted forward.

But at that instant a small but heavy patch of cloud drifted across the face of the moon and the light went out like a snuffed candle.

And when the cloud had passed, the speeding trio were practically out of range. On the faint chance of a lucky hit, he emptied the magazine, only to see them, apparently unharmed, vanish into the blackness of the canyon. There was no doubt in his mind but that they would keep on going.

Reloading the Winchester and holstering it, he sent Shadow forward to where the dead man lay. Dismounting, he knelt beside the body, peering at the distorted face that looked familiar. He passed a hand across the left shoulder.

Yes, it was tightly bandaged. The fellow was the hellion who tried to rob Chris Ames and later escaped from the Gunlock calaboose. Well, his robbing days were over. That is unless such things were permitted in Hades, which Slade rather doubted.

The dead outlaw's horse was standing patiently near-by. Slade quickly removed the rig and turned it loose. The body he left where it lay. It could be taken care of later. He would have enough trouble with the herd without being burdened by it.

Before turning his attention to the cattle, which, pretty well worn out by a long and fast run across the range, had quieted and were grazing, he emptied the dead man's pockets but discovered nothing of significance save a good deal of money, which he replaced. After which he mounted, rolled a cigarette and sat smoking, meanwhile keeping a watchful eye on the canyon mouth, although he had little fear of the outlaws returning. He'd let the cows rest a bit before starting them on their homeward trip.

Getting the critters rounded up and headed in the right direction was something of a chore for a single rider, but with Shadow's help he succeeded. Once they were moving they gave him little trouble.

The rose and gold of the dawn had given place to almost full day when Slade permitted his weary charges to pause in the vicinity of the Walking H ranchhouse. It was about time for everybody to be stirring, so he did not hesitate to hammer on the front door until he gained admittance.

It was Manuel, the cook, who opened the door

to stare, then bow low. As Slade entered, old John himself came bumbling down the stairs, barefooted. He, too, stared.

"Slade!" he exploded. "What in the blankety-blank brings you in the middle of the night?"

"I just rolled in a few of your beef critters that came close to getting themselves lost in New Mexico," Slade replied. "They're outside on pasture okay, only I'm afraid they lost a little weight last night."

Harper gulped and goggled. "Son, will you please tell me what in the blinkin' blue blazes you're talking about?" he begged.

Slade told him, in detail. Old John sat down heavily. "Son," he said slowly, "I guess I'm mighty beholdin' to you. I was figuring to round up those cows today and start them moving to market; they're contracted for. I plan to use the money to meet an installment on that blasted note that's due in a few days. Without it, I'd be in trouble."

"Well, they're already rounded up for you," Slade chuckled. "You can thank the hellions for that, at least."

Harper permitted himself a smile. "Yes, I'm sure beholdin' to you," he repeated. "That would have just about ruined me."

"I don't think you need worry about being ruined, Mr. Harper," Slade told him cheerfully. He gestured to the west.

"Over there somewhere," he concluded, "is a horse wearing a rig, and a body hooked to the stirrup, if he hasn't managed to shake the hellion loose. Please send somebody to look after the horse and pack the carcass in, and the other one over by the canyon mouth. And send somebody to notify the sheriff; I don't feel up to the ride to town right now."

"Take care of it right away," Harper replied. He flung open the door and let out a few bellows. Everybody was up now, and the wrangler with whom Shadow was acquainted had already looked after the big black. Harper relayed the orders and came back to his chair.

At this juncture, Manuel hurried in with a cup of steaming coffee.

"And *Cápitan*'s breakfast will be ready in the very short order," he promised and ambled back to the kitchen.

Old John regarded *El Halcón* fixedly for a moment. "Son, Manuel has been telling me things about you, and I set a heap of store by Manuel's judgment," he said. "He figures you are just about right-hand man to the big boss up above. He says you are always showing up where folks are having a tough time and that when you trail your twine, everything's taken care of and hunky-dory. I've a notion he's plumb right."

"I hope he is and always will be," Slade replied soberly.

"He is, and he always will be," Harper repeated with conclusive emphasis.

After breakfast, during which old John regaled the hands with a vivid rehash of the night's happenings, he said to Slade, "Now you for a spell of ear pounding; to bed with you."

Slade obeyed orders and slept soundly until past noon. When he descended to the living room, he found Lank Jim Sanborn there and proceeded to do a little serious talking.

"Jim," he told the range boss, "from now on I don't want John to ever be riding around alone. Be with him at all times; better still, have a hand or two along. And keep him away from the hills."

"You really think those hellions might take a shot at him?" Sanborn asked.

"I do, definitely," Slade replied, the full force of his pale eyes on the range boss's face. "We can't afford to take chances."

"Okay," sighed Sanborn. "I'll follow your lead, no matter what it is. I think he'll listen to me."

"If he doesn't let me know at once," Slade said. "If you consider it best, tell him you're doing what I told you to."

"I will," Sanborn promised. "I know darn well he'll listen to you; but I've a notion I've got enough savvy to put it over. He sorta likes company, which will make it easier.

"By the way," he added, "the boys located those bodies and the horses and brought 'em in;

170

carcasses are laid out in the barn. Want to take a look at them?"

"After the sheriff gets here," Slade answered, sipping the coffee Manuel had brought him. "I imagine he'll show up any time now."

Sheriff Young did arrive within an hour and the story of the night before was repeated for his benefit.

"Thinning 'em out! Thinning 'em out!" he commented, nodding his grizzled head with satisfaction.

"Yes, but the head of the outfit is still running loose," Slade answered, repeating something he had often said before, "and that sort of a head grows a new body mighty fast. Until he is corraled, we can still expect trouble."

"Just a matter of time," said Young. "Well, I'd like to take a look at those carcasses."

The second body, which had been dragged across the prairie for several miles, was pretty well banged up, but after a good look, Slade remarked, "I'm pretty sure this is the other of that pair that tried to drop the stick of timber on my head."

"All present and accounted for!" chuckled the sheriff. "This one looks like he had a whole carload dumped on him. Good work, horse!

"I'll arrange with John to have them packed into town and we'll put 'em on exhibition, just in case," he added.

"Not a bad notion," Slade agreed, "although it's doubtful if anything comes of it."

After a cup of coffee and a snack, Young asked, "And now what?"

"Now I guess we'd better head for town," Slade decided. "Mr. Harper," he said to old John, "in the next few days I'd like to have you talk with somebody I'll bring to see you."

"Be plumb glad to," Harper answered.

As they got under way, Young asked, "Going to bring Dave Benedict for a conflab with John?"

"Yes, very shortly," Slade replied. "I think it's about time to start things moving. I'll decide just when after a word with Benedict. I can't see as it will do any harm in the light of recent developments."

The sheriff nodded. "Looks that way to me, especially now you've got Lank Jim riding herd on Harper."

After a period of silence, he remarked, "And you still figure you haven't anything on Lane?"

"Definitely not," Slade replied. "I'm morally certain he was one of the three that escaped last night, but moral certainty doesn't go in court. There you have to have proof and, unfortunately, I have no proof of any wrongdoing on the part of Craig Lane. Oh, he's a slippery customer, all right, and he seems to always get the breaks. To make them, rather. He moves fast and aside from a couple of slips, always in the right direction."

"Uh-huh, but I'll warrant he makes one move too many before long," growled the sheriff.

"Yes," Slade conceded, "but in the meanwhile any moves he makes may well be fraught with danger to somebody. He's a cold killer when he feels it is to his advantage to kill."

They rode in silence, Slade experiencing an uneasy premonition that they would hear of Craig Lane's next move before long, and unpleasantly.

He was not wrong.

17

It was almost full dark when they reached Gunlock. After stabling his horse, Slade proceeded to the Walking Beam for the scolding he felt sure was in store for him.

He didn't get one; Dolores was too happy to see him back safe to give him a going-over for his extended absence. Not until they sat down to dinner together did she ask for an explanation.

Without reservation, Slade told her, knowing she would be getting a very likely garbled account from others. She shook her curly head and sighed.

"What a life of violence you lead," she said, and that was all.

In addition to her impulsive Spanish blood, Dolores Cameron had quite a bit of the canniness of her Scotch ancestry and knew when silence was more effective than speech.

A couple of uneventful days followed, during which Craig Lane did not put in an appearance at Gunlock. Slade took advantage of the quiet to ride the range north of Sinking Creek to determine the best spot for Dave Benedict, the oil man, to set his drilling rig.

Confident he would be able to swing John

Harper into line, he had several talks with Benedict and told him to make ready to very shortly begin operations.

As the days passed, Slade grew increasingly restless. The uneasy premonition that trouble was brewing persisted, became stronger. The most irritating angle was that he had not the slightest notion what Lane might have in mind. That he was keeping a close watch on developments, doubtless including all activities around the Walking H ranchhouse and its environs, he felt sure. And very likely he had one of his men stationed in Gunlock to keep an eye on things in town.

Finally, the morning of the third day, *El Halcón* paid a visit to Dave Benedict.

"What do you say we ride up to the Walking H *casa* and have a talk with Harper?" he suggested.

"Suits me," agreed the oil man. "I'll get my horse."

As they rode across the range, Slade pointed out salient features. On the lip of a rather wide and deep hollow he drew rein.

"Here's where you'll set your drilling rig," he said. "The hollow provides a natural reservoir to take care of the overflow until you can get the well capped and storage tanks built."

"You figure she'll be a gusher, then?"

"She will be," Slade replied confidently. "The seepage that formed the Gunlock pool indicates that this is a high-pressure area. Yes, you'll get a gusher, one you may have trouble controlling."

"We'll control it," Benedict predicted cheerfully. "Let 'er blow, high, wide, and handsome!"

They rode on, Slade marvelling at the beauty of the autumnal vista. Already the grass heads were tipped with amethyst that smoldered in the sunlight. The hollows were bronzed with the fading ferns. The hills were warrior monks clad in scarlet and gold, marching in serried ranks to give losing battle to the advancing white legions of the frost. Canyons and ravines were swathed in mystic violet crowned with flame. In denser thickets the already withered leaves were flakes of dead gold, the brighter for the shadowy depths behind.

To the seeing eye and the understanding heart, death is as fair as life, decay as growth. Which truth impressed itself more and more on Walt Slade as he viewed the exquisite loveliness of the land he revered and served.

Old Dave Benedict, wise in men and the ways of men, doubtless understood what was passing in his young companion's mind, for he smiled benignly and refrained from speech.

Without incident, they reached the Walking H *casa*, where they found a wrangler pottering about the yard.

"Mr. Harper in?" Slade asked.

"Nope," replied the wrangler. "I hitched up the

buckboard for him and he set out for Medford about two hours ago; said he had business at the bank."

"Sanborn with him of course," Slade stated rather than asked. The wrangler shook his head.

"Nope," he repeated. "Jim's out on the range with the boys. The Boss went it alone."

Slade stared at the man. His eyes were the color of frosted steel, his face set in bleak lines, but his voice was quiet when he said, "I believe he would drive east by south until he strikes the trail which parallels the Cap Rock and then turn east, right?"

"Uh-huh, that's right," replied the wrangler. "That's the best way to get to Medford from here."

Slade gave a shout— "Manuel!" The old cook came running.

"Manuel," Slade introduced the oil man, "this is Mr. Benedict. Look after him till I get back."

"Of a certainty, *Cápitan*," the cook replied. Slade turned to Benedict.

"Dave," he said, "stay here till I return."

"Where in blazes are you going?" asked the bewildered driller.

"I'm going to try and overtake Harper while he's still alive," Slade replied grimly. "Get going, Shadow!"

The big black whirled in response to Slade's knee pressure and headed east by south, steadily lengthening his stride, leaving Benedict to stare and mutter.

"Now, feller, it's up to you," Slade told the horse as he settled himself in the saddle. "If you can't make it, a good man is going to die. We've got to catch him before that trail veers in close to the Cap Rock and the breaks that extend out from its base, or shortly after. I don't know where they'll plan to lay for him, but it'll be somewhere in that neighborhood. I'll wager a hatful of pesos that somebody has been keeping tabs on the ranchhouse, and that the rest of the bunch isn't far off. So it's up to you."

As he rode, Slade estimated the start Harper had. The light buckboard would travel fast over good ground, and old John had the reputation of being a fast driver. Also, he would very likely be anxious to reach the bank before the closing hour. So he was probably around fifteen miles ahead of the speeding black at the moment.

Not too bad, Slade felt. He watched his mount closely, listened to his breathing. Shadow was gradually increasing his speed and getting his lungs to working properly. Slade waited a little longer, then his voice rang out, "Trail, Shadow, trail!"

Shadow knew what that meant and reacted accordingly. He snorted joyously, slugged his head above the bit and poured his long body over the ground. His steely legs surged back and forth like steam driven pistons, his irons drummed the soil. He knew very well he was taking part in some sort of a race and strained his eyes to catch a glimpse of whatever the devil was in front of him. Never mind! Whatever it was, it had to be overtaken, and passed. He set his whole soul in the task that confronted him.

Swaying easily in the saddle, Slade encouraged him with voice and hand, keeping his head well up for the time being, gradually slackening the reins while he talked soothingly to the straining cayuse. And he strained his eyes for a sight of the bouncing dot that would be the buckboard, and the gray ribbon of the Cap Rock Trail.

He sighted the trail first, as he expected to. And a few minutes later, Shadow's hoofs rang on its surface.

Now the going was even better than across the grass-carpeted prairie, for the track was in good condition and comparatively free of stones. Shadow's racing speed increased even a little more.

With his eyes, Slade constantly swept the prairie to the north. He was of the opinion that the outlaws would circle around to get in front of the buckboard before staging their drygulching. And if he could sight them before they entered the breaks, the rugged and broken terrain that footed the Cap Rock, through which the trail would later run, his task would be simpler. He eased Shadow a little and continued to scan the rangeland to the north.

The trail was veering steadily toward the breaks and the level track was giving place to dips and rises, still slight, but with steadily increasing height. Now and then his view to the north would be broken by juts of rock that abruptly spired upward. Slade began to grow acutely uneasy; it seemed to him that he should have gotten a glimpse of the buckboard before now.

Suddenly to the north and far ahead appeared four absurdly tiny mannikins mounted on toy horses, or so they looked to be at the moment. Both men and horses would quickly grow plenty large as Shadow closed the distance. Slade tensed for action and strained his eyes for his second and more important quarry, the buckboard.

Now the trail was close to the breaks and soon would merge with their rough and craggy contours. He glanced toward the speeding horsemen, who were veering more and more to the south. Shadow was gaining, but they were still far to the east.

The trail dipped into a shallow hollow, then climbed a gentle sag. Shadow reached the crest and Slade saw, uncomfortably far ahead, a bouncing blob that he knew was the buckboard containing John Harper.

His gaze shifted toward the four horsemen and he muttered under his breath. They were veering sharply toward the rugged terrain that now edged the trail. They appeared to be just about opposite the lurching vehicle and drawing ahead of it. Slade loosened the bridle and Shadow, freed from the restraining hand, lunged forward. Slade calculated the distance; it was going to be close. He had to get within something like decent shooting distance, did he hope to prevent the devils from accomplishing their murderous design. He spoke to Shadow and the straining black increased his flying speed still a little more.

Now the outlaws were well ahead of the buckboard and were entering the fringe of the breaks. And now men and horses had assumed almost full size, and the buckboard had taken on definite shape. Slade was not sure whether the band could spot the vehicle from their present location, although they would undoubtedly soon be able to.

He thought of firing a warning shot in the hope of attracting Harper's attention, but refrained. Old John, not knowing what the devil it was all about, would be more likely to speed up instead of slowing down or halting. Also, it would notify the outlaws of his presence, which he certainly did not wish to do at the moment.

Fortunately the sharp dips and sags of the breaks to the north were devoid of vegetation and from the slightly higher elevation of the trail he could still keep the devils in sight.

That favorable condition would not prevail for long, however. No great way from where they rode began clumps of thicket which would provide them with concealment. Slade began to estimate the distance that separated him from the bunch. More than a thousand yards; he'd have to get closer than that. A grim race, with a life the stake.

Shadow still closed the distance, a little more, a little more. The outlaw band, which had been hidden for a moment, came into view atop a ledge that overlooked the trail. The buckboard was descending a sag into a shallow hollow and for the moment was out of their sight; but once it topped the rise its occupant would be at their mercy, and they would show no mercy. He couldn't wait any longer.

At six hundred yards, Slade opened fire from the back of his speeding horse. He could see the outlaws plainly, but they could also see him. He prayed the buckboard would keep in the clear for just a few minutes longer. At a word of command, Shadow had levelled off to a smooth running walk.

The outlaws whirled to face the Ranger as the slugs from the Winchester whined past. Flickers of flame showed pale in the sunlight as they returned the fire.

Slugs fanned Slade's face, but weaving and swerving, he rode on into the storm of lead.

A bullet burned a red streak across his neck and hurled him sideways with the shock. Another ripped the shoulder of his shirt. A third wobbled his hat on his head. The outlaws had an advantage in that they were stationary while he was shooting from a moving stance. On the other hand, their target was also moving and they were outlined, hard and clear, against the sky.

The distance shrank from six hundred yards to five-fifty, and Slade's eyes and the high-power Winchester took toll. A man slewed to one side and fell. A moment later a second joined the first on the ground. The two remaining whirled their horses and went skalleyhooting down the slope. Slade jerked Shadow to a halt and lined sights with one, tall and broad-shouldered. He squeezed the trigger, and the hammer clicked on an empty shell!

Muttering a disgusted oath, he slammed cartridges into the magazine and fired three more shots at the fleeing pair. But they were out of range of anything but a lucky chance hit, and the luck didn't hold that far. Slade watched them dwindle out of sight into the north, then spoke to Shadow and rode on to where the buckboard had halted at the bottom of the sag, old John huddled on the seat thoroughly bewildered and more than a little frightened.

"Slade!" he shouted as he recognized the Ranger. "What in blazes is going on?"

"You loco old shorthorn!" Slade stormed at him, for he was far from in a good temper, "didn't I leave orders for you not to be mavericking around by yourself! If you weren't old enough to be my father, I'd haul you out of there, turn you over my knee and spank you till you couldn't sit down!"

Later, old John said to Jim Sanborn, "For a minute I was scairt he was going to do it anyhow."

To Slade he replied meekly, "I figured you meant not to go prowlin' around on the range. Didn't think there'd be any harm in just drivin' to town."

"If I'd gotten here a few minutes later and you had reached the top of that sag before I did, you'd have found out how much harm," Slade countered grimly. "All right, forget it and let's get going; I want to see what I bagged."

The "game" proved to be nothing out of the ordinary so far as looks were concerned. Of medium size with hard-lined faces, nothing to distinguish them from the average range rider. Their pockets disclosed nothing of interest, save money, which Slade replaced.

"Outlaw scum," was Slade's verdict. "I doubt if they were original members of the bunch; the sort a leader enlists when he's getting desperate, in my opinion. We'll leave them where they are and let the sheriff pick them up if he's a mind to. Wait till I get the rigs off those two horses; then we'd better be moving if you hope to reach the bank before closing time. I suppose you're packing that money you got for the cows?"

"That's right," old John admitted sheepishly.

"Would have made the hellions a nice haul in addition to their main objective, which we will discuss later," Slade said. "Let's go!"

18

Without further adventures or misadventures, they reached the quiet cow town of Medford. With the horses cared for, they repaired to the bank.

"No mention of what happened today, please," Slade requested as they entered the building. "It would require explanations I'm not ready to make."

"Just as you say," agreed Harper. "How about the herd the other night? I'd like to tell Manning about that."

"That'll be okay," Slade replied. "It's common knowledge."

Slade was introduced to the elderly bank president, who glanced somewhat askance at the tall Ranger's bullet burned neck, the hole in his hat and his ripped shirt. However, he shook hands cordially enough.

Harper he greeted with warmth and evident relief.

"Sure glad you made it today, John," he said. "There was a directors' meeting yesterday and I came in for some censure for having so much paper out with land for security; you know the land condition in this section right now. Yes, I'm sure glad you made it."

187

"If it wasn't for him, I wouldn't have made it," Harper replied, jerking his thumb at Slade.

"How's that?" asked the banker.

Old John told him about the widelooped herd Slade had retrieved, and the story lost nothing in the telling. The bank president shook hands again.

"John is lucky to have such friends," he said. "Sure hope you can make it in next month, John."

"I'll do the best I can," Harper answered wearily. Slade spoke.

"I think I can assure you, sir, that Mr. Harper will have no difficulty meeting his obligation," he said.

The banker looked puzzled, as much as to say, "What do *you* know about it?" But the pale cold eyes meeting his apparently caused him not to put his thought into words. What he did say was, "I'm glad to hear you say that, Mr. Slade. What do you think, John?"

"I think," Harper replied, "that if he says it, I'll borrow more money to bet on it."

"And," smiled the banker, "I'll borrow money to bet you'll win. Thank you, Mr. Slade.

"John," he added in a graver voice, "I'm doing all I can for you, but I'm bucking the stockholders and the board of directors in this matter, and they have the power to overrule me. And I'll have to admit they're dubious about the whole business. So please don't make any slips.

Everything depends on your ability to meet that note when the final big payment falls due. Don't forget."

"I won't, and there won't be any slips," Harper declared confidently.

After they left the bank, old John said, "Now what?"

"Now," Slade suggested, "suppose we tie onto something to eat, let the horses rest another hour or so and then head for home. Be late when we get there but there is somebody waiting at the *casa* I want you to speak with. Among other things, it'll explain what happened this afternoon."

"Suits me," agreed Harper. "I know a place where we can get a good surroundin', and a snort. I feel the need of one right now, and you sure ought to. How's your neck? Didn't bleed much."

"I'd forgotten all about it," Slade replied. "Guess I'll have to put on another shirt, though; this one is a mite airy."

"And your hat, too," chuckled Harper. "The chance you took, out there in the open swappin' lead with those four sidewinders!"

"I had the element of surprise on my side," Slade deprecated the feat. "That's important and gave me a certain advantage."

Old John snorted and didn't look at all convinced.

It was long past dark when they reached the Walking H *casa*, to find everybody, including

Dave Benedict, in a decidedly perturbed state of mind. Only Manuel, the old Mexican cook, had remained calm.

"Where *El Dios* smiles, there walks *El Halcón*, and those he protects," he said to the worried Benedict.

A comforting word of confidence the oil man never forgot.

Old John, with the true eloquence that comes not from the mind but from the heart, related the story of the stirring happenings on the trail to an eager gathering that insisted, when he had finished, in shaking hands with Slade, one and all.

After which he and Slade and Benedict held a serious consultation. When all the details were laid before him, Harper said, "Well, I never did like the smell of the blasted stuff, but I reckon I can put up with the smell better than I can losing my holding. Okay, Benedict, fifty-fifty, eh? If Slade says so, I'll do it, and here's my hand on it."

The partnership was ratified by a handshake. That was all. It lasted for years and involved the handling of much money, but it was never put in writing and was never violated, in the spirit or in the letter, by either man.

After a good night's rest and a hearty breakfast, Slade and Benedict headed for town, the latter bubbling with enthusiasm over his latest project.

"Guess I'm just a wildcatter at heart," he chuckled. "I'm doing all right with my Gunlock holdings, but the notion of opening up a new field has got me jumping. If a real gusher comes in, I'll be whoopin' like a school kid with the home team winning. I can't wait to get started."

Slade was also in a fairly complacent frame of mind, for he felt he had accomplished something. However, he was far from being completely satisfied. He still had a chore to do. So long as Craig Lane and what was left of his bunch were active his task was not finished. And he began to fear that Lane, feeling the jig was up, might decide to pull out of the section, which might well mean a long and arduous chase. For it was axiomatic that a Ranger never gave up the trail of a criminal. Craig Lane had violated Texas law and must be brought to justice, via the hot end of a bullet or the noosed end of a rope.

They found Gunlock its usual turbulent self. Benedict hurried on to the field. Slade, after stabling his horse, entered the Walking Beam, where he found, as he expected, Dolores anxiously waiting for him.

She exclaimed over his bullet-scorched neck, and although he made light of the injury, which was really quite slight, she insisted on treating it.

"There, that's better," she said. "Now I'll get

you some coffee, and when you're hungry, let me know. Mr. Ames isn't in right now but he'll soon be back."

As he drank the coffee, she sat in silence for a while regarding him with her big eyes.

"Walt," she said at length, "just why are you so set on keeping up a feud with those awful men? Are you one of Sheriff Young's deputies? People seem to think you are."

After a brief hesitation, he replied, "I'll expect you to keep the dainty latigo tight on that very pretty jaw."

They were alone, so he drew the silver star set on a silver circle from its secret pocket and handed it to her.

She studied it for several moments, apparently not particularly surprised, before returning it to him.

"Guess it could be worse," she said. "At least you're not just chuckline riding around with no place to go. So perhaps some time you'll think of a place to come back to."

"I certainly will," he promised.

She smiled, a trifle wistfully. "And now I'll fix you something to eat, with my own hands," she said and trotted off to the kitchen.

Just as it is axiomatic that a Texas Ranger never gives up a trail, it is axiomatic that an outlaw leader must keep his followers supplied with ready cash if he hopes to hold them in line. Walt Slade knew this and there was no doubt in his mind but that Craig Lane knew it also. So it was logical to believe that, with his exchequer needing to be replenished after several frustrated attempts to do so, Lane would strike someplace and soon. Slade was cudgeling his brains in an endeavor to anticipate the shrewd devil's next move when Sheriff Young entered and joined him.

"Well, what's happened?" he asked as he sat down and motioned a waiter.

Slade told him. The sheriff swore in a weary voice.

"Okay," he said resignedly, "I'll fetch the carcasses in. Trail a drunk by empty bottles! Trail you by empty bodies! Just as simple as that. And you managed to swing Harper into line, eh?"

"Yes, he agreed to string along with Benedict," Slade replied. "I'm confident he'll never have cause to regret it."

"Guess that's right," agreed Young. "And he can thank his lucky stars that you showed up in the section."

"He's not completely out of the woods yet," Slade observed. "Little doubt in my mind but that Lane will make another try for him, if he can just figure a way to do it. Anyhow, Harper won't be mavericking around by himself any more for a while; he got a good scare thrown into him."

"And you still don't figure you've got anything on Lane?" the sheriff asked.

"Once again I'm convinced he was one of the pair that got away, but I couldn't prove it," Slade answered. "You can't recognize features at six hundred yards, and Harper never got a look at him at all."

"The ornery sidewinder!" Young growled as he gulped the drink the waiter brought him and gestured for a refill. "The hellion sure gets the breaks."

"But I figure I helped him get the last one," Slade said. "I should have counted my shots and not gotten caught with an empty magazine right when I needed one most. Guess I was a mite excited."

"Oh, sure!" the sheriff snorted derisively. "You should have set down with a pencil and paper and figured it all out, with blue whistlers singing songs to you."

At that moment, Dolores reappeared convoying a waiter who bore Slade's meal. She smiled and dimpled at the sheriff.

"Cooked it my own self," she said. "How about you, Sheriff, will you have something?"

"If *you* cook it, I'll even eat sheep," the sheriff responded gallantly. Quite a concession on the part of a former cattleman.

"You won't have to," Dolores laughed. "You'll

get just what Walt has." She returned to the kitchen.

"She's quite a gal; they don't come any better," Young chuckled. "Purty as a spotted dog under a little red wagon, too. You're darn lucky."

Slade did not argue the point.

While Slade was eating, Chris Ames came in. He waved a greeting and hurried to the back room. A few minutes later he reappeared and made his way to the table.

"Just saw Dave Benedict," he announced. "He's worked up as a hen with a settin' of ducklings and busy as a packrat in a jewelry store. Just wait till the boys at the field learn what he figures to do. They'll turn handsprings and say he is out of his mind."

"Uh-huh!" snorted the sheriff. "And a lot of folks said he was out of his mind when he drilled the first well down at the field. Didn't take him long to shut 'em up. Trust old Dave not to miss any bets. And with Slade backin' him, I just wish I owned a slice of John Harper's land."

19

Dave Benedict wasted no time. The following morning, the surprised citizens of Gunlock saw a train of big freight wagons loaded with materials roll north across Sinking Creek.

They came to rest at the point on the edge of the hollow designated by Walt Slade as the drilling spot. Saws rasped, hammers thudded, and a tall derrick began to rise. Gunlock seethed with excitement, and there were violent arguments in all quarters. The majority of the oil men agreed that old Dave had cracked up at last, had gone plumb loco. They pointed out that the natural slope was from north to south and that any oil that might have once been under John Harper's land would have long since drained into the Gunlock reservoir. Benedict mentioned the contention to Slade.

"Quite logical reasoning, only it is not borne out by the geological facts," *El Halcón* replied. "What they don't know or can't understand is that all indications are that once, perhaps a million years back, the slope was reversed. Then the rivers flowed north into what was then a great inland sea. Terrestrial convulsions changed the surface slope. The rivers flowed south instead of north. The sea dried and formed the salt and alkali deserts.

"But the great fundamental anticline did not reverse but held its trend of south to north."

"Anticline?" Benedict interrupted, looking puzzled.

"An anticline," Slade explained, "is an upfold or arch of stratified rock in which the beds or layers dip in opposite directions from the crest."

"I see." Benedict nodded his understanding.

"The crest of the anticline," Slade resumed, "is well to the south of the Cap Rock. Oil south of the Cap Rock follows the southward slope of the anticline which extends under the Gulf of Mexico.

"Because of which," he interpolated thoughtfully, "the time will come when drilling will be conducted off-shore, well out in the Gulf. And the presence of off-shore oil claimed by Texas, the terms of the treaty of annexation setting the Texas off-shore limit at twelve instead of three miles, will, I venture to predict, result in a hot political row between the Federal Government and Texas. I doubt, however, that it will take place in our time.

"To get back to the original subject. As I told you, the Gunlock pool is the result of terrific subterranean pressure exerted chiefly on the surface of the main reservoir, which is at a much greater depth than the Gunlock pool. All you have to do is keep on drilling and you'll hit it."

"I'll keep on till I hit China, then I'll build a

tower and keep going," Benedict declared cheerfully. "I have perfect faith in your deductions, so let the blabbermouths spout. We'll show 'em!"

The blabbermouths did spout, but the wiser and more experienced of the oil men refused to be drawn into the argument. As one remarked, "Old Dave don't miss any bets, and that young feller Slade is smart as a treeful of owls; he knows more about the oil business than all of us put together. Wonder what he really is and where did he come from?"

"Some folks say he's an owlhoot."

"That so? Well, he sure don't cotton to others of that brand, the way he's been workin' 'em over since he landed here. Sheriff Young swears by him, and old Blount is another one who don't miss many bets."

But as the ponderous bit churned deeper and deeper into the earth with no results, the voices of Benedict's detractors grew louder and even those who supported him grew slightly dubious.

"Remember what folks said about Tony Lucas who brought in the first well of the great Spindletop field at Beaumont," Slade reminded him. "Down more than eleven hundred feet without any positive indications. And then right when not even Lucas expected a strike just yet, it happened, and Spindletop was in."

"Just what's going to happen here," declared Benedict. "And, incidentally, it's the easiest drilling I ever experienced. Any rock we encounter is all shattered and busted up and the bit goes through it a-whoopin'." Slade nodded sober agreement as he watched iron casings being sunk into the bore while the bit was changed.

Yes, so far as the well was concerned, Slade was confidently optimistic. Otherwise he began to experience an annoying sense of frustration. He had not been sent into the section to drill oil wells but to apprehend certain malefactors, and so far as that was concerned, he felt he was getting exactly nowhere. Craig Lane did not put in an appearance at Gunlock and there were no indications that he was active anywhere in the section.

"Wonder if the horned toad has pulled out?" asked Sheriff Young in the course of a conversation with the Ranger.

"I still don't think so," Slade replied. "May be just a hunch, but I'm of the opinion that we will be hearing about him in one way or another, and soon." The sheriff looked dubious.

Another day drew peacefully toward the close. That is, as peacefully as a day ever was in unpeaceful Gunlock.

And then, most unexpectedly, Craig Lane, assured and debonair as usual, strolled into the Walking Beam where Slade and the sheriff were eating their dinner. He waved a cordial greeting, smiled his derisive smile, and sauntered to the bar.

For a moment, Slade thought Blount Young was going to have a stroke.

"Easy!" he cautioned. "Take it easy. Don't give him the satisfaction of seeing you paw sod; he's having enough fun as it is. Take it easy and eat your dinner as if nothing happened."

The sheriff raised his coffee cup in a shaking hand and took a swallow, and very nearly strangled.

"The nerve of that sidewinder!" he gasped. "Walkin' in like he owned the joint."

"And there is nothing we can do about it," Slade said. "As I've told you a number of times, I have absolutely nothing on him, and he knows it as well as I do, even though he may suspect I'm not exactly what some folks say I am. Eat your dinner."

The sheriff tried, although it seemed each bite might choke him. Slade pondered Craig Lane's broad back.

"I wonder why he did it?" he remarked to his companion. "Just to show off? I doubt it. Blount, I've a notion there's something back of his putting in an appearance this way. What? I haven't the least idea, but I have a feeling we'll find out before long."

They did.

Just a couple of minutes later, a man in the blue cloth and brass buttons of a passenger trainman rushed in, glared wildly about, and fairly ran to the table.

"Sheriff!" he panted, "They want you down at the station, right away."

"What the blazes—" Young began, but Slade interrupted.

"Let's go," he said, rising to his feet. "I've a feeling this is going to bear me out."

Stares followed them as they hurried to the door, but Craig Lane did not turn his head. Slade wondered if he was smiling, and thought he very probably was.

"Now what in the devil is this all about?" demanded the sheriff as they reached the outside. "Why do they want me at the station?"

The trainman had caught his breath and spoke coherently.

"The Northwest Limited," he said. "It was robbed."

"Robbed!" exploded Young.

"That's right," said the trainman. "Express car robbed. I gather they got between thirty and forty thousand dollars, bank shipment."

"Did they wreck the train?" asked Young. The trainman shook his head.

"Nope, worked it slicker than that."

"Suppose," Slade suggested, "you start at the beginning and let us know just what happened."

"We were highballing along about fifteen miles east of town when somebody pulled the signal cord and stopped the train," the other explained. "The conductor opened a door and looked out and saw four fellers on horseback slide out of a patch of brush alongside the right-of-way and go riding off across the prairie. The engineer was yelling to him that he thought they got off the train. He didn't know what it was all about, but we were late already, so he waved the hogger to go ahead and went on through the coaches trying to find out what happened and couldn't learn anything. When he got through the head coach and to the express car, he tried the end door which was supposed to be locked. It wasn't. He opened the door and went in and found the messenger tied to a chair and gagged."

"Was he injured?" Slade asked. The trainman again shook his head.

"Nope, he was all right," he replied. "But the safe door was standing open. The con got the messenger loose and the gag out of his mouth. He said he was working at his little desk when the door he swears was locked opened and four fellers with black cloths over their faces and guns in their hands walked in. He didn't argue with them."

"Which was lucky for him," Slade interpolated. "Go on."

"Nope, he didn't argue with them," the brakeman repeated. "They tied him up and one squatted in front of the safe and worked the combination slick as a whistle. They cleaned out the safe, putting the money in sacks they carried, told him to keep quiet and walked out the back end door, shutting it after them. Just a little later he heard the signal whistle and the train stopped. That's all he knew till the con came in and cut him loose."

"How far from town was the train when it stopped, did you say?" asked the sheriff.

"About fifteen miles, I reckon," the brakeman replied. "The con got over the tender to the engine cab and told the hogger what had happened and he highballed to get here quick as he could."

"Fifteen miles," repeated the sheriff and turned to Slade.

"Guess that lets *him* out," he said meaningly, apropos of Craig Lane. "He never could have ridden that distance and got here before the train. Was just a little after train time when he came into the Walking Beam. Yep, I guess that lets him out."

"Do you think so?" Slade asked.

"Why, sure," replied Young. "Don't you?"

"I do not," Slade said. "Explain why later. Well, here's the station; perhaps we can learn something more."

They didn't learn much. The express messenger

and the conductor confirmed the brakeman's story and had little to add to it.

"The man who opened the safe, did you notice anything in particular relative to him?" Slade asked the messenger.

"Why, no, nothing much," the messenger answered. "He was sorta big and tall—taller than the other three, I'd say."

Slade turned to the conductor. "And the four you saw riding away, did you note anything outstanding about them?"

The con shook his head. "I didn't pay much attention to them till the hogger started yelling," he admitted. "If one was taller than the others I didn't notice it. They were sorta humped over in their saddles and it was already beginning to get hazy."

"Well, guess you'd better start rolling as soon as the dispatcher will clear you," Slade said. "Nothing more you can do here, and you're already plenty late."

The conductor nodded and hurried to the telegraph operator, who had already sent word of the robbery over the wires.

Outside the station, Young asked, "Just what did you mean by what you said a minute ago?"

"I mean that Craig Lane was the man who opened the express car safe," Slade replied.

"But—but," sputtered the sheriff, "four men robbed the express car and then rode away."

"So it would appear, but appearances can sometime be deceptive," Slade replied. "This is an excellent example of that truism."

"Won't you please tell me what you're talking about before I go plumb loco and start climbing the walls," the sheriff begged. "If it was Lane opened the safe, how could he have gotten here as soon as the train did?"

"By way of the train," Slade replied laconically. "Don't you see it, Blount? The men who robbed the express car got on the train at some station over east. At the proper time, they, doubtless one by one, slipped out of the head car and onto the blind baggage. Nobody would have paid them any attention. Lane was one of them. He opened the express car door with a key he'd probably made from a wax impression. He and the others had slipped on masks. Lane had already proven himself an expert cracksman who could do anything with locks—something we formerly didn't have to contend with in this section. That old box would have posed no difficulty to him. Remember this is the second time a safe has been opened that way hereabouts."

Slade paused to roll a cigarette as they walked slowly along the street, then resumed.

"They had everything planned to the minute, knew just where to stop the train. Lane had removed his mask and just before he pulled the signal cord, he had doubtless passed through the head car without anybody paying any attention to him. Between the head coach and the second, he pulled the cord, walked into the second coach and sat down. Everybody would be wondering why the train was slowing to a stop and again he would have attracted no attention."

"But the four who rode away?" the sheriff reminded plaintively.

"Three of them were the men who helped Lane in the express car," Slade explained. "They dropped off the train as it slowed and dived into the brush, where a fifth man waited with their horses. Lane came on to town on the train, thereby providing for himself just about a fool-proof alibi. Oh, it was a smooth piece of work. Can't say as I ever heard of a smoother. Now he can stick around town as long as he desires and gather information for his next raid, if he intends to make one, which I consider likely. Even did someone recall seeing him on the train it would mean nothing. Do you see it?"

"Yes, I see it," growled the sheriff. "I've a prime notion to plug that sidewinder on general principles."

"Better be sure to make it look like an accident, otherwise you might end up wearing your hair short, staying in at night, and making hair bridles for the State," Slade smilingly advised. "Remember, Craig Lane is looked upon as a prosperous businessman of good repute, and so far there's no proof that he isn't. Come on, let's go finish our dinner."

When they reached the Walking Beam, they found Dolores waiting for them.

"Sit down," she said. "I threw out what you hadn't finished and ordered you a fresh meal. Can't you even take time off to eat?"

Craig Lane was not present when they entered. Nor did he return that night.

20

Slade spent most of the next morning wandering around Gunlock. He dropped in at several places, listening to scraps of conversation, studying faces. Around noon he visited Bob Evans at the Buzzard Bait saloon, chatted with him for a while, and learned nothing.

Nowhere did he encounter Craig Lane. He thought that very likely the hellion had a rendezvous somewhere with his followers, for the purpose of dividing up the express car loot.

Well, Lane was sitting pretty now, so far as money was concerned. There was a chance that, after his big haul, he might pull out of the section. However, Slade did not believe he would just yet.

Leaving the Buzzard Bait, he made his way to the Walking Beam for a bite to eat and a talk with Dolores. After which he stood at the edge of town for a while, gazing north toward the spidery outline of the tall derrick with its jigging walking beam, its cable rising and falling, and its ponderous bit churning downward through the soil. Benedict was more than nine hundred feet down, now, well below the depth of the Gunlock Field. His detractors were making derisive remarks, and those who still had faith in his judgment had largely fallen silent.

It was mid afternoon when Slade got the rig on Shadow and rode north to the scene of the drilling. As he dismounted, Benedict came hurrying to greet him.

"Come along," said the oil man, "I want you to hear something." He led the way to the bore, and gazed expectantly at *El Halcón*.

Up from the dark depths rose a sound different from any that had preceded it. The slithering mutter of the bit churning through earth had been replaced by a hard drumming that vibrated the air. A sound that Slade instantly recognized.

"You're hammering cap rock," he said. "Just as I expected. I figured you'd hit it at about nine hundred. Better change your bit. And keep everybody who doesn't have to be here away from the bore. I think it will be some time yet before you break through, but if she happens to come in unexpectedly, like Lucas's well did over at the Spindletop Field, she'll blow everything sky high. You'll have casings and chunks of the rig all over the landscape. Don't take chances you don't have to; a gusher like this one promises to be may well prove deadly."

The experienced oil man understood and took all precautions possible.

After watching while the bit was changed and again listening to the muffled thunder rising from the depths of the earth, Slade rode back to town through the purple mystery of the dusk.

He was very well satisfied with the progress of the drilling, but with his own progress not at all. Craig Lane was still very much on the loose, and so long as he was mavericking around, trouble could be expected.

Fortunately, the express car robbery had been consummated without murder as a side line; but had the messenger made a single false move, it would have been curtains for him. Lane's next strike might well have a more deadly ending.

Oh, the devil! Slade shrugged his broad shoulders and headed for the Walking Beam. Dolores would be there, her soft voice would be soothing, and in her company he would forget his pressing problem, for a while.

"So you're really sticking around, for a few minutes at least," she said when she joined him. "I thought when Mr. Ames told me you were riding out of town that you were off on another wild adventure and I wouldn't see you for a week."

"How could I stay away except when I really have to?" he protested.

Dolores shrugged daintily. "Oh, after all, a woman is only a woman," she retorted.

"And the mightiest force in the world, at any rate where the majority of us poor men is concerned," he returned smilingly.

"Sounds nice, but I doubt it," she replied.

Slade spent a very pleasant evening at the

Walking Beam, mostly with her for company, and when closing time arrived, he was much more relaxed, just about his normal optimistic self.

But even communion with his charming companion could not altogether banish the uneasy presentiment that something was going to happen.

Something did, and soon. Something unexpected and disturbing.

Early the following afternoon, Slade rode north to the site of the drilling. He studied the surroundings of the spot, more as a matter of habit than anything else, as he approached the site. Several straggles of thicket partly hid the lower section of the derrick and the rig floor. Not until he was close was the whole operation in view. He dismounted and approached the derrick.

Benedict sauntered forward to meet him. He shook his head disapprovingly.

"The blasted stuff is hard as steel," he said, referring to the cap rock the bit was pounding. "May take us days to get through it, depending on how thick it is. We'll make it, though, just a matter of time."

Slade moved onto the rig platform and listened intently with his unusually sensitive ears.

"Dave," he said, "of course it's just a guess on my part—impossible to tell for sure—but I have a feeling that rock is not very thick. Seems to me the vibratory accompaniment to the pounding of the bit tends to bolster such an assumption."

"Okay, whatever that means," sighed Benedict. "Sometimes I can't understand half you say. I gather, though, that you mean we are liable to bust through at any time."

"Exactly," Slade agreed. "As you said, it may take days. But then again it may be but a matter of hours. I hope so, for the time element is gradually becoming important."

"Yes, I can understand that," Benedict replied. "John's note falls due mighty soon and anything that would delay us might cause him trouble." Slade nodded agreement.

"I'm keeping the hoisting engineer on the job tonight after the regular quitting time," Benedict said. "I want to keep that bit pounding all night without a letup. The rest of the boys will knock off for a few hours of rest and then be back here shortly after midnight, just in case. They don't mind getting double time for just loafing around."

"A good idea," Slade said, "and the chances are I'll be sort of keeping a watch on things till you get back."

An hour or so later, four horsemen were observed riding swiftly from the north. They quickly proved to be John Harper, Lank Jim Sanborn, and two of the Walking H hands.

Harper dismounted and strode to where Slade stood. He appeared to be in a very bad temper indeed.

"Look at this!" he rumbled, shoving forward a sheet of embossed stationery.

Slade took it and his black brows drew together as he read.

Dear John:

I told you I would do all I could for you, but I'm afraid I'll have to tell you that things have gotten out of my hands. As I mentioned, the stockholders and the board of directors have been very dubious about the situation as it stands. Especially since pessimistic reports have been coming in from the oil field.

So when an offer was made to buy your note, they overruled me and snapped it up. As you know, such a note is negotiable and can be sold or bought. It is not even necessary for the bank to notify the mortgagor of the sale, but of course I am notifying you at once.

The note was bought by a Mr. Craig Lane who, I understand, is in business at Gunlock.

Really, however, I can't see that the note changing hands will make any difference to you, for my faith in you and Mr. Slade is unshaken. You'll be able to meet the obligation when it falls due, of that I am positive.

The message was signed by Wilford Manning, the president of the Medford Bank.

"What the devil does it mean?" Harper demanded of Slade.

"I don't know, but I don't like it," the Ranger replied. "That smooth devil has got something up his sleeve, on that you can rely. What? I haven't the slightest notion, yet. On the face of it, it would appear that Manning is right, that it really makes little difference to you who holds the mortgage. All we have to do is get the well in, which I'm confident we will in plenty of time. But Lane must know that. So why the devil did he buy the note? A question to which I sure wish I had the answer."

"You'll get it," Harper said confidently. "No doubt in my mind as to that. Well, seeing as I'm down here, I think I'll spend the night in town. Don't worry, the boys will be with me every minute."

He mounted and the quartet headed for Gunlock, old John in a much better temper after his conflab with Slade.

El Halcón, however, was far from in an equable frame of mind. Why had Craig Lane bought that note, very likely with the money from the express car robbery? Could be just a gamble on his part? Slade did not think so. It was almost as if Lane knew something nobody else did. But what?

Once more Slade listened to the muffled thudding rising from the depths of the bore. It seemed to him there was an added ring to the steady beat.

"Be on your toes," he cautioned Benedict. "I feel she may come in any time. Remember, the first Spindletop well came in without the slightest preliminary warning, while they were changing the bit and everything was quiet. Could happen here. Like the proverbial straw that broke the camel's back, any little thing could provide the added small jar that will bust the cap."

After a final glance around, Slade headed back to town, puzzling over the latest development.

"It's like waiting for the jigger upstairs to drop the other shoe," he told Shadow. "Now I'm in worse shape than I was last night. Oh, well, we'll just have to wait and see which way the cat jumps."

A not very satisfying decision, cats being most undependable critters.

21

Slade ate his dinner at the Walking Beam, chatted for a while with Harper, Lank Jim, and Chris Ames, had several dances with Dolores, trying hard to get into the spirit of things, and failed signally. He was restless and uneasy.

A couple of hours before midnight, he left the saloon and wandered about the streets. But the constant din of voices and Gunlock's hullabaloo in general irritated him. He arrived at a sudden decision.

Better to be out on the lonely prairie by himself, where at least it was quiet and peaceful. And soon Benedict's boys would be heading for the well site and there might be things to do. He got the rig on Shadow and rode slowly north.

A custom of long habit, he instinctively kept the straggles of thicket and other growth between him and his objective, although there was really no reason to do so, so far as he knew. Before long he could hear, in the hush of the night, the sound of the hoisting engine and the jigging walking beam. Everything appeared to be under control.

He was nearing the last bristle of growth, which was close to the derrick, when the drone of the engine and the clank of the walking beam abruptly ceased.

217

"Now what's that jigger shutting down for?" he wondered as he reined in at the edge of the thicket to listen. He thought he heard a low mutter of voices.

In men who ride much alone, with danger a constant stirrup companion, there grows a mysterious, seemingly unexplainable sixth sense that warns of peril when none apparently is present. That sense was highly developed in *El Halcón* and he had learned long ago not to ignore its message.

And now that voiceless monitor was setting up a silent but urgent clamor in his brain. He listened another moment, then swung to the ground.

"Stay put, horse," he said and glided into the belt of growth. Careful not to make the slightest noise, he wormed his way to the outer edge, which was just behind the shed that housed the engine. And now the sound of voices was plain. He eased forward, hugging the wall of the squat building and almost fell over something on the ground. He bent down to examine it.

Two flares burned on the rig floor and by a trickle of light he saw it was the body of the engineer, blood still oozing from an ugly gash in his scalp. Slade felt of his heart. It was beating, not too feebly; he'd have to wait a bit for attention. Straightening up, Slade crept forward until he could peer around the edge of the shed.

Just mounting the rig floor were five men,

one carrying a bundle of something which he hugged close. The full light of the flares fell on the face of the foremost, and the Ranger instantly recognized Craig Lane.

And *El Halcón* understood!

He drew both guns and stepped forward, keeping as much in the shadow of the shed as possible. His voice rang out.

"Elevate! You're covered! In the name of the State of Texas!"

There was a yelp of alarm. For an instant the five outlaws froze. Then Craig Lane's right hand, with marvellous speed, flashed to his left armpit.

But before he could draw the shoulder gun, Slade shot him, twice. Lane gave a strangled cry and fell forward on his face. The night blazed with gunfire.

Ducking, weaving, slithering, *El Halcón* answered the outlaws shot for shot. A slug ripped his shirt sleeve. Another tore through the leg of his overalls, just graining the flesh. A third pierced his already much abused hat.

A man fell. But there were still three on their feet, shooting as fast as they could, getting the range. The odds were too great. Slade squeezed both triggers; he'd take as many with him as he could before he went down.

A blinding flash of light, the boom of an explosion! Slade was hurled backward and almost off his feet by the concussion. A slug had hit the bundle of dynamite one of the outlaws carried, the dynamite intended to cave in the well bore and delay the drilling for weeks.

Slade caught his balance, took a step toward the shattered rig floor and the drunkenly leaning derrick.

There was a deafening roar. Tons of casing pipe were projected through the rig floor and high into the air. The derrick flew into pieces. Slade scooped up the body of the injured engineer and ran for his life as a hissing black column, glinting in the starlight, spouted up and up and up! Higher and higher! Full two hundred feet!

Chunks of derrick thudded to the ground all around the burdened Ranger. One that weighed about half a ton fanned his face with the wind of its passing.

There followed a pattering as of summer rain as the wind-frayed plume of crude oil reached its height and fell in a shower of black gold to flow into the big hollow that formed a natural storage tank.

Slade gently placed the engineer on the grass. He was rolling his bloody head from side to side and muttering with returning consciousness. A moment later he opened his eyes and stared dazedly at the Ranger.

"What happened to you?" Slade asked.

"Don't know for sure," the other mumbled. "Guess some hellion slipped up behind me and belted me one. I didn't hear anything, didn't see anything but a big blaze of light. That's all I remember till I saw you bendin' over me. What in blazes happened around here? I was just gettin' my senses back and it sounded like an earthquake."

"Just a little old gusher came in," Slade told him cheerfully. "Now lie still till I get some stuff from my pouches and patch you up a bit."

He stood up and whistled a loud and musical note. A couple of minutes and Shadow came charging through the growth, snorting inquiringly.

From his pouches, Slade took a roll of bandage and a jar of antiseptic salve. He probed the vicinity of the wound with his sensitive fingers and concluded the damage was negligible. Then he smeared the wound with the salve and deftly bandaged it.

"That'll hold you for the time being," he said. "We'll have Doc Cooper look you over later. I think you can sit up, now."

The engineer did so, swore feebly, and puffed with appreciation the cigarette Slade rolled for him.

Now Gunlock was thoroughly awake. Men on horseback and on foot were sloshing through the waters of Sinking Creek and racing across the prairie to the booming gusher.

Foremost were Dave Benedict's workers who had gotten an early start. They raised a wild cheer, turned handsprings, pounded each other on the back, whooping and yelling.

Gunlock Field Number Two was in!

Benedict galloped up, his face one great grin. He dismounted, viewed the scene with pardonable pride, drew Slade's head down and shouted in his ear. Slade straightened up and his great voice rolled in thunder through the tumult.

"Boys, Mr. Benedict requests me to tell you that after you get the darn thing capped and under control, there'll be a full month's pay, as a bonus, for everybody!"

An even wilder cheer greeted the announcement and the workers cut fresh capers.

The torn and battered bodies of Craig Lane and his followers were located and removed. John Harper arrived on horseback and joined Slade and Benedict.

"Lane's plan was to drop the dynamite into the bore and cave it in," Slade explained for his benefit. "That would have delayed the drilling until long after your note he held would be due. Nothing new about the method—it has been used before in the case of feuds between rival oil men. Would have worked, all right, if I hadn't had the luck to intercept it."

"Luck!" snorted old John. "I got another name for it! And mighty soon, me and Dave are going to talk business to you."

Slade smiled and did not comment.

It took many hours of frantic labor to bring the gusher under control with a firmly-anchored valve. Meanwhile the big hollow was full to the brim.

After the chore was finished, many of the oil-drenched and exhausted workers went to sleep right where they were. But in the late evening, freshly scrubbed and glowing, all were lined up at Dave Benedict's office to receive their promised bonus.

To celebrate the event, Benedict had also given a substantial bonus to the workers on his other projects, and these winsome gentlemen, with the ready cooperation of others, proceeded to show Gunlock the wildest night the oil town had ever known.

In the Walking Beam, Dave Benedict and old John clicked glasses with Chris Ames, and talked over the stirring happenings of the past twenty-four hours.

"Where's Slade?" Harper suddenly asked.

"Dunno," replied Benedict. "Prowlin' around somewhere, I reckon. He was here a little while ago."

Dolores could have told them, for she, his kiss still warm on her lips, had watched him ride away, tall and graceful atop his great black horse, his face ashine with pleasant memories, his eyes fixed on the far horizon, heading to where duty called and danger and new adventure waited.

| Books are produced in the United States using U.S.-based materials | Books are printed using a revolutionary new process called THINKtech™ that lowers energy usage by 70% and increases overall quality | Books are durable and flexible because of Smyth-sewing | Paper is sourced using environmentally responsible foresting methods and the paper is acid-free |

Center Point Large Print
600 Brooks Road / PO Box 1
Thorndike, ME 04986-0001 USA

(207) 568-3717

US & Canada:
1 800 929-9108
www.centerpointlargeprint.com